THE DARKNESS OF
THE BODY

by the same author

THE GHOST OF HENRY JAMES

SLIDES

RELATIVES

David Plante

THE DARKNESS OF
THE BODY

JONATHAN CAPE
THIRTY BEDFORD SQUARE LONDON

FIRST PUBLISHED 1974
© 1974 BY DAVID PLANTE

JONATHAN CAPE LTD
30 BEDFORD SQUARE, LONDON WCI

ISBN 0 224 00933 8

PRINTED AND BOUND IN GREAT BRITAIN
BY RICHARD CLAY (THE CHAUCER PRESS) LTD
BUNGAY, SUFFOLK

TO MY MOTHER AND FATHER

THE DARKNESS OF
THE BODY

He couldn't sleep the first night out. He walked the deserted deck, his back against the wind. He saw a woman standing by the rail where the wind blew strongest. Her hair was thrashing in tangles. She looked at him, but she turned away, her hand over her mouth, as he passed her.

He sat in a deck-chair and folded the lapels of his overcoat over his chest. The long dark view before him was of the open sea.

He saw the woman over the next days. He couldn't associate her with anyone in particular. Even at her table, which he had to pass to get to his, she sat quietly.

At his own table, he glanced often about the half-empty dining-room multiplied by the mirrors. The voices of the passengers, merging into a hum, never rose above the reverberations from the engines. When the talk at his table fell, the sound of the engines swelled up, and he listened to it. Four tables away, he saw the woman, who also seemed to be listening to the resonant vibrations.

He got to know an elderly woman who was at her table. He brought her a cup of tea. He asked, 'The young woman at your table –'

'The quiet one,' the elderly woman said.

'Yes.'

'I thought you might ask about her. I ask myself about her. I'm not sure she isn't rude for never expressing a spark of interest. Her husband, on the other hand –'

'Her husband?'

'Yes, the tall blond man at our table.'

He met the tall blond man at the bar. The man was the only person there, and he held on to the edge with one hand to keep himself from lurching. Valerian grabbed on also. He ordered a drink; when placed before him, it sloshed over the rim. The blond man said, 'We must be in a storm.'

'Perhaps we can out-do it,' Valerian said, and raised his glass to the man before drinking.

The man laughed. He held out a broad hand. He said his name was Jonathan Rack. Valerian Chambers introduced himself. He felt in Jonathan Rack's strong grip a slight pull towards him, and Rack's smile expressed an openness which, having drawn Valerian into it, left them both wondering what to do. Valerian searched the room.

His eyes stopped at the doorway where Rack's wife was standing, looking about. She appeared to step back when she saw her husband speaking to someone; she and Valerian exchanged looks, and he was struck by her eyes. She came over, her husband said, 'This is my wife,' but Valerian knew he could not talk with her looking at him. He left, and went into the winter garden to finish his drink.

The rocking rolled him from side to side in his bed. He could hear, in the darkness, the rattling of the tooth-glass and the water decanter in their metal holders, and the air raging through the vents. It was only the motion that let him know he was at sea.

He wondered why he should find himself attracted to someone he had simply looked at, about whom he knew nothing.

Jonathan was alone when Valerian next saw him. Valerian said, 'I think the storm has turned away from us.'

Jonathan smiled, but there was a dark ring around the smile as there were dark rings around his eyes.

'Is this your first trip?' Valerian asked.

'Mine, not my wife's.'

'Has she travelled?'

'In the past. She didn't really want to travel now. I thought she should. I wanted her to have a change.'

'That's why you're travelling?'

'Yes. For a change.'

'Where will you go?'

'All over. I know it's not the best time to travel now, but I couldn't have made it any other time. We have the whole winter.'

Valerian suddenly couldn't keep up the conversation. He simply looked at Jonathan, who, his lips drawn into a thin smile, looked over his head at the other passengers on the deck.

Jonathan said, 'I'd better go see if she's ready for dinner.'

On his way through the dining-room Valerian noted that the place across from Jonathan was empty. From his table, he kept looking to see if his wife had arrived, and once caught Jonathan's eye; he saw in it that his wife wouldn't come, and he also saw that the reasons for her staying away were hardly more known to her husband than to him. Jonathan didn't respond to Valerian for a moment, and when he did his smile was strained.

Alone in his cabin, Valerian took out of a valise the objects he had bought abroad. Among them, wrapped in a handkerchief he untied, were brass pendants. He held them up: a triangle, a square, a circle. They shone. Reflected in them, he saw an eye, a cheek, an ear, a mouth.

Jonathan approached him the moment he stepped into the lounge.

Valerian said, 'Your wife – I haven't seen her today.'

'She's in the cabin. Last night was rough.'

'The rocking.'

'No, it's not the rocking. She doesn't like travelling.'

'She's difficult, is she?' Valeria asked, half laughing.

Jonathan looked at him as though this had never occurred to him. He said, 'Not really. She always agrees to do what I think might be best, even if it doesn't appeal to her, though I'd like to do what appeals to her.'

There was a pause, and both men withdrew a little from one

another until Valerian said, 'If you took a flat, then you wouldn't have to travel, but you'd still be in a different place.'

'I'm sure I couldn't afford that.'

'That depends on where you look. You could get a small flat near where I live. It's not central, and the buildings aren't well cared for, but there's a park.'

Jonathan's eyes appeared to go out of focus as he looked at Valerian, as if he were trying to imagine the flat, the neighbourhood, the park, in the middle of Valerian's forehead.

Valerian was again introduced to the wife the next time he saw her, not by name, but, as before, almost off-handedly: 'My wife.' They ordered mid-morning coffee. The three sat around a table. It was obvious that the wife had not wanted to come, but agreed to because Jonathan asked her to. Each time Valerian turned to her, she gave him a quick smile and drew her hand through her hair. Jonathan told her, as he no doubt had done before, of Valerian's idea that they should find an apartment and stay, and she smiled.

'Shall we, then?' Jonathan asked.

Again, she only smiled. Then they fell silent. Valerian drank his coffee. His attention was pulled down to the engines, which made everything on the ship vibrate as though from a high-pitched sound, sometimes too high-pitched to hear, but always perceptible. He felt it trembling at his fingertips in the handle of his cup, felt it in the chair, felt it under his shoes. He imagined that the vibrations, from deep down, kept them all together and going: a dark ship on a dark ocean.

He gave them addresses of some friends, he recommended his bank for transfers of money, he helped them to get a place to stay at the far end of the drive in which he lived. Once they were installed he heard nothing from them.

In the late afternoon, he crossed the park on his way from work. The dusk was turning to darkness. In the distance were bare trees about which the mist rose. As he crossed a grey wet playing-field a bell began to clang.

A woman in a dun uniform riding a bicycle passed him on a

path. The thin wheels splashed. She said, 'We're closing the gates.'

'Yes, I hear the bell,' he said, but the park-keeper was out of earshot.

The bell continued to ring, and thousands of small birds shrieked in the bare trees and bushes. He heard from far away, intermingling, faint traffic noises and a factory whistle, the barking of a dog, and a fog-horn on a river barge.

The path brought him under the trees to a part of the park enclosed by large wet rhododendron bushes, where there were empty parterres and benches. The path twisted, and other paths branched off from it.

He saw a woman coming towards him. He recognized her at once as Mrs Rack. He wondered what he should say to her when he passed her, but she turned off the path on to another.

There was no reason in the world he could think of why he couldn't simply follow after her, stop her, and talk to her, except that he felt she wouldn't want it.

When he got to the gate, the lady park-keeper was standing beside it, a key in her hand. She closed the gate after he left; she locked it with a chain and padlock.

He should, he thought, tell her there was still someone inside, but he couldn't bring himself to, as if that would give her more trouble than she was willing to handle at the moment. She rode off on her bicycle and he crossed the street and entered his mansion block, but the image of the woman wandering about in the locked-up park stayed with him like an echo.

He wondered if he should ring her husband. That they had not got in touch with him meant that they wanted to have nothing to do with him, so he thought he could not ring; but his mind kept circling about the telephone and he knew it wouldn't let go until he picked it up and dialled. He did. Jonathan Rack answered in a low voice, perhaps a little surprised that someone had rung.

Valerian said, 'I'm sorry to disturb you. I wouldn't have –' He paused.

'I'm sorry,' Rack said, 'who's speaking?'

When Valerian mentioned his name, the response was as if jerked up by a sudden 'Oh!'

Valerian said, 'I saw your wife a short while ago in the park. She probably didn't know that the gates are locked after dark; I think she was locked in.'

'I see,' Jonathan answered, but nothing more.

'I didn't speak to her, but I did see her.'

After a long pause, Jonathan said, 'I'd better go out to find her.'

'You'll have to jump over the fence.'

'There may be a park-keeper around still.'

Valerian said, 'Shall I help you?'

'No, thank you. I can do it. I'm sorry to be abrupt; I'd better go now.'

When he hung up, he thought: to hell with them. He'd shut them out of his mind.

But he went to the window and looked down at the park, which was dark and still.

He didn't see them after, and did shut them out of his mind. Passing the block in which he had got them a flat, he thought that they must have gone away, were travelling after all.

He himself went away for a while, this time by aeroplane.

Before he left he had asked a friend if there was anything he should see in the city where he had never been, and the friend gave him an address. He arrived to find a small theatre, where he bought a ticket and went into a very small, hot auditorium – rather, a room with chairs and mats on the floor and a platform at the front on which a woman, her long arms gesticulating in long arcs, her garments sticking to her with perspiration, was, though she seemed hardly to move, dancing. The room was full. He had to stand. There was a strong acrid smell plus a heavy smell of scent, a redolent smell as of rotting flowers and sweat. The air in the room appeared saturated with heat mist, and the men in it – all men – sat with the stillness and inertia of people not only too hot to move, but who no longer could move. Valerian stood back. No one turned to look at him, but he did not feel, either, that they were ignoring him as an intruder; no one there seemed to care about him. It was only a short while before he realized what drew their attention beyond caring, about him, the heat, the smell: not simply the slow, very slow, at times hardly seen movements of the dancer as she jutted out her chin or placed one long hand over the other, but the low, constant *ching-ching, ching-ching* of the bell on a ring about her ankle. He had only to listen to it himself for minutes – though, after, his sense of minutes elongated and contracted like the slow shifting gestures and steps of the dancer – before he, too, found himself not feeling the heat, not smelling, not seeing the men (though in a way aware of them hunched up on mats or leaning forward on chairs, some of them with their heads resting in their hands and not looking at the dancer), but only conscious of the *ching* as the dancer lightly stamped her foot. It went on and on. None of the spectators moved, and neither did Valerian. He ceased, too, to hear the sounds.

He went to his friend's barely two hours after his return to the city where he lived. He knew there would be a number of people gathered, most of whom he would know, and they would treat him as they always had. Nothing of what he had seen while away would show in his eyes, not the thinnest reflection.

The door to the flat was ajar. He took off his coat and went to the sitting-room, from where voices sounded.

He paused at the door. People in small groups were moving from one point of the room to another. Valerian searched for Ronald Ghee, his friend.

They spotted one another at the same time; Ronald came towards him, leaving a gap in a group with whom he had been speaking, and through the gap Valerian saw, motionless, leaning towards one another, Jonathan Rack and his wife.

Ronald drew him into the room by the hand. He said, 'I'm glad you're back.'

'I wasn't gone so very long.'

Ronald smiled. 'It was to me.' He paused, staring at Valerian's eyes. 'You saw the dancer.'

'Yes. Can you tell?'

'Of course,' Ronald said. He brought Valerian to a table where there were bottles and glasses. 'I hope now you'll stay here.'

Valerian suddenly put his arm over Ronald's shoulders. 'For a while.' He took his arm away to reach out for the drink Ronald had poured him. He asked, 'How do you know those two?' He indicated Jonathan and his wife with a nod of his head; they had not seen him.

Ronald turned. 'They said you had given them my name. I invited them.'

'Oh yes,' Valerian said.

'You don't recall?' Ronald asked.

'Yes, yes. I just wondered if they might have got here in another way. Have you spoken to them?'

'A little. She's not well.'

'Did she say that?' Valerian asked.

'No. I could tell.'

'She's not well in what way?'

Ronald said, "I can't believe you don't see it.'

'Yes, I do,' Valerian said quickly.

He approached them. They seemed to jump apart when they saw him. Jonathan's brow furrowed. He said, 'We tried to ring you. We wondered if something had happened. We rang your friend to ask, and he said you were away.'

'I thought you might have gone away as well.'

Jonathan's wife smiled. 'We did.'

'Far?'

'No, not too far.'

Valerian turned away from her.

He left them to talk to friends, but he kept glancing at them over the shoulders of the people around him. He saw Jonathan lean close to her, his hand on her shoulder. She whispered to him, he whispered back, and she went out.

Valerian couldn't bear to see Jonathan standing alone. He joined him. He asked, 'Has your wife left?'

'Yes,' Jonathan said.

'She's very beautiful.'

'She has beautiful eyes.'

'Isn't she well?'

'Why do you ask that?'

'She left so soon.'

'Did she appear unwell?'

Valerian frowned. 'No,' he said.

Jonathan went for another drink.

Valerian spoke to a few other people, then put down his glass to go. When he reached the door, Jonathan pushed his way to him.

'I'm sorry,' Jonathan said. 'You were right. My wife is not well.' He paused. 'Will you come? Will you see us?'

Valerian went to their flat.

Jonathan closed the door softly after Valerian stepped in and took him to the dim sitting-room. He said, in a low voice, 'She thought she should stay in her room. I'd have rung you to tell you not to come, but I hoped up to the last minute that she might change.'

'That's all right,' Valerian said.

Jonathan went out to prepare tea, and Valerian looked about the small room where nothing reflected the personal tastes of either Jonathan or his wife, as the flat had been taken furnished. He sat in a big armchair by the fire. The silence was very deep. He lay his head against the chair-back and closed his eyes – closed them it seemed to him over the whole dark winter Sunday afternoon.

The minute sounds of cups and spoons, milk jug and sugar bowl jostling one another echoed as in an immense space when Jonathan came in bearing a tray. He set it down on a little table before the fire.

'We'll let the tea brew a bit,' he said.

17

'Oh yes,' Valerian said. It was comfortable, he thought, to think about the tea brewing. He knew that Jonathan didn't want to think of anything else for the moment. There was an intimacy in their mutual reserve; the area between them swelled out with the smell and steamy warmth of the tea in its pot.

Beyond this, however, Valerian's attention was brought to the silence around them. He could not imagine anyone else in the flat, in bed, or sitting in another room. It occurred to him that Jonathan's wife was not there, had gone out, perhaps to the park, and apart from him and Jonathan the flat was as empty as the afternoon.

Jonathan said, 'I think it should be strong enough.' The tea streamed from the spout. As he was handing Valerian a cup, he pulled it back and turned about sharply. Behind him, his wife came into the room.

'Marion.'

She went straight to Valerian, her hand extended, and it seemed to him that her large eyes were spinning. She drew away from him and sat in an armchair on the other side of the fire.

'Would you like a cup of tea?' Jonathan asked her.

'Yes, please,' she said. Her voice was hoarse.

Valerian tried to examine her closely, but each time he looked towards her, she caught his eye and jerked her head up and to the side to smile. Her raised hands were supported by the fingertips resting on the arms of the chair. Her hair was partly undone. Each time she caught his eye, he had to turn away.

He still believed that she had not been in the flat, but had been somewhere else. She had, he thought, returned from somewhere he could only guess at, and her gestures, her hair, her voice suggested nothing he could even guess at. He didn't know where she had been or what she had done, but he felt, as he had felt when he had last seen her at the party, as he had perhaps felt, he now thought, the first time he'd seen her, that she had travelled far, too fast and too recklessly for her husband or him to keep up with her.

She said nothing, yet everything Jonathan and Valerian said, and said with the intention of pulling away from her presence, was pulled into her presence. Everything they said and no doubt thought gravitated to the overwhelming awareness that she was the centre of their special attention because she was not well. This was as deep and as penetrating as the surrounding silence which drew his mind out to it: she was not well.

Jonathan handed her a cup of tea. She leaned forward to take it, and the way she looked at the cup as she brought it to her made Valerian wonder if she was not seeing the cup, but a barely shaped and raging gas. And then, when she looked at him over the rim as she tipped the cup up to drink, he realized he could not be sure that she was seeing him as he was either. Their eyes crossed for a second, long enough for him to feel that she took him in completely, and he saw himself appear for the second upside down, refracted in the irises of her eyes. It startled him.

Jonathan said, 'Wouldn't you care for more?'

'Thank you,' Valerian said, and thrust his cup out. He watched Jonathan pour the tea, watched the tea steam, and, with the cup back in his hand, watched the round rim of it. He almost saw the silence encroaching about the rim in waves.

Jonathan said, 'We were saying –'

Valerian wanted to say, 'You needn't force yourself to talk.' But Jonathan did force himself to talk, and all the while he spoke Jonathan looked from the corner of his eye at his wife.

Valerian suddenly turned to her. 'Do you like living here?'

All the muscles of her face appeared to struggle as she smiled. 'In this country?'

'Yes,' he said.

She retained her smile. 'I haven't seen much of it,' she said.

'We haven't had much chance to,' Jonathan said, and took over the talk, as if, Valerian thought, he was not sure his wife wouldn't somehow close it up tightly, and he wanted it to remain large and free. Valerian hardly heard what he said. He turned again to Marion. He said, 'Wouldn't you want to?' He could sense Jonathan's tenseness as they both waited for an answer.

'I don't see the point of it.'

'Well, there's hardly any point to sight-seeing, except to see what one hasn't,' Jonathan said.

She smiled at Jonathan crookedly. 'There's nothing I haven't seen that I want to see,' she said.

Jonathan quickly said, 'But why don't you give it a chance?'

Her smile became more crooked. 'Give what a chance?'

'What you haven't seen.'

She looked at Valerian. 'Jonathan thinks it will make a difference to be in a different place, among different people and monuments. It doesn't.'

The blankness with which she said this was reflected in Jonathan's face. He took up the pot and went out for more hot water.

Left with Marion, Valerian sat back and drank the rest of his tea.

He felt, as before, that she was taking in everything about him, his clothes, his slightest movements, his expressions; not that he imagined she was interested in him; he didn't for a second sense from her any personal interest, but rather a vast, a cold, a deeply impersonal attentiveness to everything around her.

He finally said, 'I'm sure there are some things here that'd interest you.'

'What?' she asked.

'I can think of one or two places. There is a very old site – '

'In the city?'

'No, in the countryside.'

'We couldn't get there, I think.'

'With a car.'

'We don't have a car,' she said.

As he spoke, he asked himself why he made the offer. 'I have one.'

In her silence, the little noises in the room became, for a moment, still, as if shadows, cast into the room by unseen things moving behind him, over him, were arrested. Her dry lips, he saw, adhered and pulled against one another as they slowly parted. Then Jonathan came in. He put the tea pot on the table, and as he sat Marion rose.

She said, 'Please excuse me.'

'You have to go?' Jonathan asked. 'I thought we might all take a walk.'

'I can't,' she said. She didn't look at Valerian as she left the room.

Valerian said, 'I offered her to drive you both to the country.'

'Did she accept?'

'She didn't decline.'

'You're very kind, but she won't go.'

Valerian heard her walking just outside the door. He thought that she might come back in, but her footsteps stopped. Jonathan half turned towards the door. She wasn't visible, but her voice, altered to an unrecognizable hoarseness, called:

'Jonathan.'

'I'm sorry,' he said to Valerian, and went out.

Valerian heard whispers, then the voice of Jonathan, who, Valerian imagined, had taken her in his arms.

When Jonathan came into the sitting-room, Valerian stood.

'I'm sure I should go,' he said.

'She wants to go to bed,' Jonathan said.

They shook hands.

'Perhaps she'll be better after she sleeps.'

'She won't sleep,' Jonathan said.

Valerian disengaged his hand from Jonathan's, where it had been held in a prolonged clutch. He said, 'Maybe you can persuade her to go to the country.'

'Oh, I don't want to have to persuade her to do anything. I want her to do what she wants.'

Walking home, Valerian thought of her in bed, thought of Jonathan sitting on the edge of the bed or in bed with her, holding her in his arms. The images struck a series of dissonant notes in him, and he wondered if it occurred to Jonathan, holding her, kissing her, drawn into making love with her, that what she deeply wanted was to be unwell, to be irredeemably unwell.

As he fell asleep, he told himself that he must not have anything more to do with them.

He found a note from Marion Rack on his hall floor beneath the mail slot when he got home from work one late afternoon. It was written on a piece of folded paper, his full name on the outside. His overcoat still on, he unfolded it and read:

I would like to accept your offer to drive us to the country, not for me, but for Jonathan.

He answered with a note. He dropped it through their mail slot. The metal flap clanked. He waited until he heard footsteps inside the flat come towards the door.

Jonathan sat in the front seat of the car next to Valerian, who drove; Marion sat in the back. The bare trees, the smooth hills, the low dark clouds passed. Jonathan talked. Marion expressed nothing, not even when, after a long drive through empty wet roads, they arrived and walked to the site.

In the midst of a flat plain, they stopped among crude arches which were listing, the large stones chipped and black and shining with the wet. All about were stones half buried in the ground. Circling the site were great mounds. Beyond the mounds were trees, and beyond these wide open stretches of plain.

They separated, Jonathan with a guide book, Marion as though wandering, and Valerian to get away from them. He went around a mound to where some excavating was being done: a long curved trench with fragments of a wall in the bottom followed the round contour of the mound. He stood close to the edge of the trench and stared down. He circled the mound and came back to the ruins. Marion and Jonathan were not visible. He stood near the arches. The wind blew through the bare trees, about the mounds, about the ruins, but it did not, for some reason of his position, strike him; he heard it like a rising and falling hum, now loud, now low, over the ancient stones.

He passed beneath the arches and went to the other side of the site. The wild bushes were wet, so he stood on a large bare stone. He wondered where Jonathan and Marion had gone. Listening to the windy hum, it came over him that something had happened to them. He went quickly to find them.

Around the mound nearest to him, he saw her. Her back was to him. She was looking out across the plain, over which the flat banked clouds hung so low they appeared a grey countryside in reverse. He was about to approach her, but stayed back. It seemed to him odd, suddenly, that he should have anything to do with her, that he should know her name, much less have driven her to this spot. No, he had nothing whatsoever to do with her, but he realized, looking at her, that he had had a reason for wanting to bring her here : he had wanted something to happen which could be used as a point of association between them. He was even a little disappointed to find his anxiety that something unpleasant had happened was without grounds. Nothing had happened.

He continued to watch her, and drew back out of sight when he thought she was turning towards him. She was searching for a stick, which she found near a tree. She dug at the ground.

Jonathan came up behind Valerian as he stood watching. He asked, 'What's going on?' and looked past Valerian to his wife.

She dislodged something from the ground, picked it up and examined it. Jonathan went towards her, and Valerian followed.

Jonathan asked, 'Have you found something?'

She held out a square stone.

'Something to remind you of the place?' Valerian asked.

She looked at him, then at the stone. He saw a confusion come over her, as though she had forgotten why she had dug it out.

Valerian asked, 'May I see it?'

She handed it to him immediately, almost threw it into his outstretched palm. It looked as though it had been chiselled to a cube. He handed it back to her.

'Oh no,' she said, 'I don't want it.'

'It's yours,' Valerian said.

'No,' she said, 'I don't want it.'

He put it in his pocket. They returned to the car.

Unlocking the door to his flat, he thought he shouldn't have asked them to come up. He didn't want her to come into his flat. He kept the hall dark as he brought them in, and wished he could keep the whole flat dark.

He left them in the sitting-room to go to the kitchen to prepare tea and eggs and toast. He could hear them speaking, but he couldn't make out what they were speaking about.

After they ate, he showed them books, prints, chips of marble, shells, old pottery he had brought back from trips. He resented his doing so. He had never before deliberately shown them to anyone. They lay about the flat, they hung haphazardly on walls, and he liked to think, when people were visiting him, that the objects extended him into dimensions which the people, though in their midst, were unaware of; they were little points of reference to him of a context he had consciously pushed further and further out to cities in remote countries, periods in remote times, cultures as different from his as possible. Marion took in everything he showed her, took it in but made no comment on it.

He showed her an old compass for making circles and curves, a bronze disc, a small finger-drum, a wooden flute, books –

He had no idea what she thought of the objects he showed

her. She didn't touch them. In her gaze, they were reduced to battered bits of bronze, chipped bits of glass and marble, torn and foxed bits of paper, splinters of wood.

There was, after she left, a flat stillness in the room. He cleared up the dishes.

He didn't see them for days, and didn't ring.

When the telephone rang, Valerian didn't answer it. He touched it. It vibrated. Whatever anticipation was raised by the ringing remained, a sonic aurora, about the telephone, when the ringing stopped.

Twenty minutes later the telephone rang again. He answered it quickly. It was Jonathan. Valerian didn't ask if it was he who had rung before; he didn't want to know; that auroral anticipation, spread out in thin bright arcs, had suggested more than the voice of Jonathan or anything Jonathan could say.

Jonathan said, 'It was very cold in the park this afternoon –'

Valerian found himself listening to the sound of his voice as though the tone alone might give an indication of what he really meant by calling.

'No doubt you're very busy,' Jonathan went on.

'Not very,' Valerian said, and then it occurred to him why Jonathan was ringing: he was waiting for him, Valerian, to suggest that they meet. He said, 'Perhaps we can have lunch.'

'Ah,' Jonathan said.

Valerian said, 'And of course Marion.'

'Yes, Marion,' Jonathan said. He hesitated. 'Shall I ask her?'

'Please.'

There was another hesitation before Jonathan put the receiver down. He came back quickly and said, a little breathlessly, 'She can't.'

Valerian didn't know if his slight sinking feeling was relief or disappointment. He asked, tentatively, 'And you?'

A sudden relaxation in Jonathan's voice made it drop in pitch. 'Oh yes, I think I can go.'

Valerian took him to a crowded restaurant where they almost had to shout to speak to one another. Jonathan gave himself up to what was outside him, and Valerian noted his attention to the people sitting at small bare round wooden tables close to their own table, to the waitresses squeezing themselves between the chairs, to the various dishes being eaten, to the mingling conversations which, if listened to all together, caused a pulsing roar.

Then, as if all the activity about them resolved itself into one point, Jonathan kept looking in one direction. Turning to look, it took Valerian a moment to realize it was a table directly across the room from Jonathan that he was fixed on, where a man and woman were eating.

The man's back was towards Jonathan; he was tall and blond, and his hair was cut and combed in exactly the way Jonathan's was. The woman, full face, was laughing. She put her hand before her mouth because she laughed so much. Her dark eyes were wide, and gleamed.

Jonathan fell silent, his attention on his round plate, for the rest of the meal.

After lunch, Jonathan walked with Valerian to where he worked. They talked, but about what had nothing to do with either of them, Valerian thought; he was aware that the deliberate distance from anything personal, even from Valerian himself, was a distance from Marion.

The next time Jonathan rang, Valerian didn't immediately recognize his voice. He knew, as before, that Jonathan was trusting him to invite him. Valerian asked, 'Do you like music?'

'Music?'

'We might perhaps go to an afternoon concert.'

Valerian wrote Jonathan's name in the space in his diary under the date he was to meet him. The image came to Valerian of Jonathan forcing himself to stand silently among a group of strangers and waiting for one of them to speak to him. He closed his diary, put it in a drawer of his desk, and the telephone rang again.

It was Jonathan. 'I won't be able to come,' he said.

'Perhaps another time,' Valerian said.

'Perhaps.'

He asked his friend Ronald Ghee to the concert – a trio of piano, violin, cello. The tuning up, the coughs, the creaking of the chair on which the cellist sat, the cracking movements of the audience, impinged on and reduced the music, Valerian thought, to dead sounds.

In the crush bar, Ronald said, 'That was flat.'

Valerian smiled. 'Flat, yes.'

'It's a mystery what makes the difference,' Ronald said.

'I suppose.'

It was a mystery, too, Valerian thought, what made the difference between a voice that suggested to him more than what the voice said, and a flat voice. It occurred to him that Ronald's voice sounded flat, and he wondered if he knew him too well.

After the concert, they walked. They walked down a deserted street with empty garbage cans.

Ronald wanted to knock the garbage cans to make them sound. He said:

'I don't suppose you'd like to come to my place.'

Valerian didn't answer at first. Ronald wondered if his voice had projected. Valerian said:

'It's late.'

'Just for a little while. You can't go home in the state you're in.'

'Am I in a state?'

'Yes.'

Valerian paused. 'Perhaps I was expecting something this evening –'

Ronald tried to laugh. 'And it didn't happen?'

'No.'

'Then come to my place.'

Valerian said nothing.

'Come on,' Ronald said.

Standing near him in the narrow elevator, Ronald watched the veins in his neck pulse.

Valerian sat as if a great weight were forcing him to sit. He slouched into the chair.

Ronald sat across from him. He knew that, to keep Valerian, he would have to create a sense of something happening.

'Tell me what you were expecting.'

'Nothing in particular.'

'Don't be evasive.'

Valerian frowned. 'I'm not being evasive. I don't know what I wanted to happen – maybe only that I would have been, however briefly, taken up by the music, and I wasn't.'

Ronald got up. He went to a table, opened a drawer, and took out a little box. Approaching Valerian with it, he took the cover off it and tilted it so Valerian could see inside: on a bed of cotton, a stone finger. Valerian lifted the finger out. It had been broken from a statue, a long smooth index finger. He held it in his palm.

The next time he saw Jonathan was with Ronald. The three men, silent, undressed in the locker room.

Ronald, unbuttoning his shirt, saw that Valerian, half turned away from him, was watching Jonathan slowly unbutton his shirt.

He saw Valerian study him as he pulled the tails of his shirt out of his trousers, so the shirt hung open as he unbuttoned his cuffs and reached down to untie his shoes and pull them, then his socks, off. Ronald duplicated the actions, but Valerian wasn't aware of him in his concentration on Jonathan now stepping out of his trousers. A slight apprehension passed through Ronald at the sight of Jonathan's long lean legs, and it occurred to him that he didn't want Valerian to see him naked. Ronald said:

'Valerian.'

Valerian turned to him.

He could only think of: 'I didn't tell you I read a review of that concert – '

'Yes?'

'It said it was brilliant.'

Valerian hunched his shoulders. He looked back at Jonathan.

Valerian was aware that he had been studying Jonathan. He half imagined that, naked, Jonathan would not be quite like other men, but he could not imagine how he might be. His shoulders sloped into long arms, his tight hairless chest, the nipples small, gave way to a smooth abdomen, a round navel, sharp pelvis, a blond patch of pubic hair, a cock with a large exposed glans that swung as he hung his clothes in the locker. He examined Jonathan with a fascination which he had to check.

He still watched him in the shower room. Jonathan's skin gleamed under the flowing water, and all his hair, on his head and on his body, streamed down as in rivulets. When Valerian turned to shut off his shower, he caught a look from Ronald, who had been showering next to him. He saw that Ronald was aware he had been studying Jonathan.

Jonathan plunged right into the pool, and Valerian immediately followed. Jonathan's long limbs took him great stretches, but Valerian kept up to him. At the far end of the pool they trod water. Valerian was about to dive under and swim closer to him, but Jonathan suddenly submerged and swam away.

Valerian climbed out of the pool and sat at the edge next to Ronald. Water ran off their bodies. Their elbows and knees touched.

Ronald said, 'I didn't know you saw Rack much.'

'I don't see him much,' Valerian answered. 'But as he and I see very few people, it may seem like a lot.'

'And his wife?'

'I don't think she wants to see anyone.'

'You're rescuing Jonathan from her?'

Valerian laughed.

'What does he do?' Ronald asked.

'He tries to take care of his wife.'

After a moment, Ronald said, 'If I were you, I'd be careful of them.'

'Perhaps,' Valerian said.

His eyes fell through the water where, gliding past his submerged feet, Jonathan's body appeared blue and green, distorted by the lapping.

'You're drawn to him,' Ronald said.

'To Jonathan?'

As soon as he said it, he knew why he was, why, now, he followed his nude body magnified in the block of illuminated water: his body was bright and frightening for his having slept through night after night pressed next to Marion.

'Yes,' he said.

Ronald smiled.

Valerian wanted to say, 'But you don't understand.' He kept silent. He felt the warmth of Ronald seem to concentrate at the spots where they touched. Neither man moved.

Valerian and Jonathan went to a song recital. The soprano stood in the middle of the bare stage; behind her and to her right was a piano and the accompanist. The singer moved her shoulders as though to settle her body. The hall went dim.

A moment later the first chords were struck, and with them Valerian felt all the dim air about him go dimmer, felt the first few notes of the music suddenly empty it and make it go black. The singer appeared very small in the blackness, and he imagined that when she opened her mouth, her voice would not be able to penetrate the great space.

Her head was lowered. She slowly raised it, and as she raised it her singing filled the hall, and the darkness became to Valerian the darkness of a vast and open night. He did not know how it happened, but he did know when it did happen – when pitch and tone threw open all his surroundings, and he was confronted with what was completely different from anything he commonly knew.

He thought: it was impossible for him to think of a world absolutely unrelated to the one he knew; he could imagine life on another planet only in some relation to his life here; he could only imagine languages in terms of languages here; he could not in any way grasp what had nothing to do with him – and yet, at moments, he knew the sense of a state that was different, to which none of the images, none of the sounds that evoked it really applied.

The singer was not singing, he thought; her own voice had detached itself from her as a person, and she was, as though she herself were music, being sung, as he and Jonathan and the other people in the hall were being sung, as the darkness about them was being sung, as all that landscape opening up in the darkness – a planet emerging with a faint whirr as it slowly spun – was evolved in the rising music.

He turned to look at Jonathan, who sat leaning out from his seat, drawn out by some strange gravity. There was no expression on his face.

When the music stopped, Jonathan appeared to be left isolated. He lurched when they got out of their seats as if he had not used his legs in a long time.

During the second half of the recital, Valerian kept looking at Jonathan, who, pulled to the music, was visibly detached from everything that didn't have to do with it.

After, Valerian felt displaced. He said he had somewhere to go, and wouldn't be returning to his flat. They stood on the sidewalk outside the hall; the afternoon had passed into a dark evening while they'd been inside. 'You can get a bus from a stop nearby,' Valerian said.

'I think I'll walk.'

Valerian warned him, 'It's not a short stroll.'

'It doesn't matter,' Jonathan said.

They parted. Valerian looked back to make sure Jonathan had gone in the right direction, but couldn't see him.

At a corner, Jonathan saw Valerian stop beneath a street-lamp and look about. He wondered if he was searching for him and was about to go back, but Valerian turned away and continued walking, and Jonathan crossed the street.

He watched a bus go by him and stop a short way up the avenue; one person got off, and he heard, faintly, the bell the conductor pushed to signal the driver to start up again. The faint bell ringing in Jonathan's head signalled his attention to all the other sounds around him: sounds not only of traffic, but other, low, rolling, twanging, hissing sounds he couldn't identify, that seemed to emanate from a long tunnel – perhaps a subway – near him. But it wasn't just odd sounds he was hearing; he realized that, in the noise, he was somehow still hearing the music. He wished he didn't. If he could close his ears the way one could close one's eyes, he thought, and block it all out, but everything around him – cars, people, pigeons, street lamps, running gutters – made sounds, and he could not draw back from them.

The bus disappeared. He continued along the avenue, skirting the edge of the sidewalk as if the kerbstone were a narrow margin to both the traffic and the pedestrians, and if he stayed to it he would be all right. He crossed a number of streets, following his straight margin. The pedestrians dwindled, but the traffic increased, and he suddenly found himself at a junction where the avenue broadened out to a four-lane highway, a flyover spanning it, which seemed to lead out of the city. The lamps were green, and the light flashed on the thousands of swiftly moving cars. The overwhelming sound was of a penetrating, ululating roar.

Nothing was familiar. He had come too far, he thought. He should have turned off. He was sure that not even a taxi, much less a bus, would come; not that he wanted a taxi or a bus, as he did not want to go back to the flat now.

He retraced his steps. The avenue appeared very long, and he was not sure at what point he should turn off from it. He did know, in any case, that he should go towards the left, towards the river. He thought he could find his way from there.

Jonathan could no longer bear the noise of the traffic and the other interpenetrating noises. When he came to a dim quiet side-street to his left he turned down it and soon, because the street sloped sharply downwards, the sounds of the avenue ceased. It was a short street, and he was quickly at the end of it; he turned left again, the street sloping yet deeper, but, instead of finding another street to the left, the street twisted to the right, and he had to follow it. It wasn't very late, but he found himself among narrow streets that were deserted, as if the people living in the thin brick houses, so squeezed together each one bulged at its front into a painful little bay window, kept hours different from the main part of the city. He passed a bicycle chained to a fence, parked cars, an old flaking rowing boat tipped upside down on the sidewalk.

He took an even narrower street, the first one in the direction of the river, he thought. It was cobbled and slanted on either side, with a gutter running down the middle of it. At the bottom, he passed beneath an arch, and out among huge warehouses.

The warehouses were very close together, hardly space between them for a truck to pass through. They were closed up tightly, with occasional pale lights seen through small dirty windows.

He hurried down a passage and came to the river front. Cranes rose above him, up into the purple night sky. A bridge spanned the river far to his left, its sharp bright lights slurs in the flowing reflections. Jonathan went to the stone barrier at the edge of the river and looked down. The river was full. A barge passed him, and, as though pulled in its wake, beams of wood, bottles, crates; houses further up the river might have been destroyed in a flood and washed down. He watched the debris pass him.

And then, slowly, he became aware again of the sounds: the striking peals of distant bells, muted sounds of traffic, low bursts of laughter, the wash and swish of the water against the stone embankment, thumps, wails, indistinguishable, far away, a dark and heavy music whose incessant and inescapable harmonies terrified him.

When he finally got back to the flat, he found Marion asleep on the divan in the sitting-room. She woke when he came into the room, but didn't rise. He sat on the edge of the divan.

'I'm sorry I took so long,' he said.

She shook her head. It didn't matter.

He took off his coat and threw it on the floor, then his jacket. He kicked off his shoes. He lay beside her on the narrow, lumpy divan. He could feel the short bristles of the upholstery rubbing against his cheek and neck. He didn't take her in his arms, but she was pressed against him, and her breathing rose as his fell, fell as his rose. He wanted to take her in his arms, but he knew she would pull away. The only light in the room was from the gas fire. The fire, blown by wind down the chimney, sounded wild and now and then shrieked – a continuation of the possessive music he could not get out of his head. He heard his voice say, 'I walked back, but I got lost.'

She said nothing.

He wanted to tell her what had happened, but he knew he would not be able to find the words; he knew he would not be able to get across to her what he now heard, and even if he tried, she would make him stop, confronting him with a total lack of any possible sense of its significance to him, to her, to anyone. She would say, 'Yes,' which amounted, ultimately, to: 'What does it matter?' How could it not matter, he thought, when it was everywhere? How could it not matter, especially to her, when she was the cause of it?

Weeks passed, and he did not ring Valerian.

Valerian dialled, and after four rings – rings which were, Valerian thought, as though at the bottom of the ocean where there was no one to hear them – the receiver was picked up, and Marion Rack said quietly, 'Yes.'

It was as though a sea creature had answered. There was no point at all to simple conversation.

She said, again, 'Yes.'

34

'It's Valerian.'

'Did you want to speak to Jonathan?'

'I'd like to talk to you just as well.'

It seemed to him that currents raced past the earpiece.

He said, 'I haven't seen you in a very long time –' He forced himself to add: ' – either of you.'

He imagined himself on the ocean floor digging into the sand with his feet, holding himself against the cold streams, trying to make their confrontation as natural as possible.

'We've been here,' she said.

A deeper, stronger current pulled at him to draw him away. He spoke against it. 'I hope you've been well.'

There was another silence from her. A moment later, however, she said, 'There's no point in speaking to me. If you want to speak to Jonathan, say so.'

He felt that he was about to be hurled down the current. He answered impulsively: 'I didn't want to speak to him.'

'No? But what reason do you have for speaking to me?'

'Must I have a reason?'

Her voice was stark and cold, and as controlled as his was not. 'No, but you're wasting your time on me.'

He didn't know what else to say. He hung up. He remained by the telephone, his pulse beating throughout his body.

He could hardly bring himself to answer the phone when, a minute later, it rang. He let it ring, again and again, the rings like insistent, abrupt screams; he picked it up to stop it.

The next day, he and Jonathan met.

Jonathan appeared thinner. He said, 'I'm sorry that she was sharp. I heard her, but I couldn't stop her. You can't stop her, really.'

'If you tried?'

'Stop her! I have tried. Over the past weeks I've tried very hard.' He put his hands on either side of his face. 'She's been bad lately,' he continued.

'Why?'

'If I only knew!'

'What's wrong with her?' Valerian asked.

Jonathan raised both his hands.

'Doesn't *she* have any idea?'

'She doesn't believe there's anything wrong. She believes she is like everybody else.'

Valerian said nothing.

'Oh, she's not mad, if that's what you suspect,' Jonathan said. 'She finds things – well – very dark.' He paused. 'She can't go on.'

'There's nothing you can do?'

Jonathan didn't say, but Valerian saw in his face, turned to look at the bare trees, what he would try to do.

Valerian thought, as he had thought many times before, but this time with an awareness that seemed to make all the air chill: he must leave them to themselves, he must stay away from them.

As he left Jonathan, he said, 'I'll be going away.'

Jonathan said, 'Yes, do.'

No one was in the churchyard as Valerian crossed it on his way to the library. The Saturday afternoon was bright and cold. He sat on a bench facing the black church. All around the edges of the yard were black gravestones. As he breathed in the cold air, he breathed in, he thought, the emptiness and stillness of the churchyard, where the winter shadows were deep and long, and the flowerbeds were wet and bare.

When two women with carrier bags came in and walked towards him, he got up, followed the cement path to the back of the yard and passed through a narrow gate into the small graveyard. The wooden gate thumped against the gatepost, and immediately, rising from the dry tangled vines hanging from the enclosing walls, hundreds of chirping sparrows flew out, circled the graves, then resettled in the vines, from which their thin shrills continued. The noise subsided after a while; Valerian went to the middle of the yard.

He took away with him a sense of cold stillness evoked in him by the small graveyard. He sensed it still in the library, though it was populated enough to make it necessary for him to manoeuvre about amongst the people to get to the books he wanted.

In one of the narrow alcoves he saw Marion, shelves of books ranged on either side of her. Valerian's impulse was to pass her quickly, but he stood back and watched her for a moment. She looked at the spines without once reaching out to pull a book down. Perhaps she wasn't even looking at the spines, but standing quietly. It occurred to him that the library or the park was her only refuge. He had never thought before that Marion might want to get away to be alone. It was a strange desire to be alone that sent her into public places, but he understood it. He left her.

As he searched the packed shelves, he was more aware of her than of the titles his eyes crossed. She was, he was aware, standing in an alcove not far from him, and he was sure she had not changed position. The book he wanted was not on the shelf. Walking to the desk to reserve it, he passed near the alcove and looked in.

As if she had been expecting him, Marion was standing full face towards him. He stopped. Valerian didn't know if she wanted him to approach or leave. He stepped towards her.

'Jonathan told me you're about to go off again,' she said abruptly.

'Yes,' he answered.

'I thought you might have left; we haven't seen you.'

'No.'

She looked at him for a moment, then said, 'You've been very kind to Jonathan. He counts on you.'

Valerian kept his voice to a whisper. 'What is it he counts on me for?'

She smiled. 'To get him away from me.'

He smiled back. Valerian realized he was, for the first time, staring directly in her eyes. It was she who switched them to the side. A second later, however, she again looked at Valerian, and it seemed to him her pupils and irises had enlarged and left very little of the whites showing. He remembered that he had once believed the pupils were open holes, and a thin object – a needle – could be passed through without at all damaging the eye; he imagined everything she looked at now – the books, the chairs, the desks, the carpets – passing through her pupils and, inside, revolving out to the edges of an empty and blue sky, as blue and as empty as her irises. He waited for her to move away.

She said, 'He's been reluctant to get in touch with you.'

'Why?'

'He thought you had had enough of us.'

'No,' Valerian said. 'I haven't seen anyone.'

'He'd like it if you came.'

'And you?'

She said, 'If I could repeat what I said to you over the telephone without being rude –'

'It's only the rudeness you regret?' he asked.

'Yes.'

'Then it is a waste —'

'Ask Jonathan,' she said.

'You've convinced him?'

Her face went blank.

He asked, 'Are you going home after you collect your books? Can I walk with you?'

She said, 'I really didn't come for books.'

He said, 'I thought you mightn't have.'

'Why do you think I did come?'

'To get away from Jonathan,' he answered.

A slight expression rose to her face; he could not be sure if she were smiling or frowning.

The lunch was prepared by Marion. She brought the food into the sitting-room, where a table had been set up. She set the dishes down carefully. Jonathan, Valerian noted, watched her carefully. He said:

'Marion went into town yesterday by herself.'

Valerian wondered if this was meant to be a good sign. He

couldn't see any response in Marion. She cleared and brought the dishes out. Valerian leaned a little over the oval table and said:

'She's better.'

Jonathan shook his head. 'No, she isn't.'

Valerian sat back. Marion returned with a cheese board. He noticed how, serving the cheese, she kept glancing at Jonathan, aware that he was watching all her smallest movements.

It appeared to Valerian that all the edges of Jonathan's skull were prominent, as if the skin were taut, making his face sharp. When he said to Marion, 'You forgot the biscuits,' Valerian imagined he saw his teeth pressing against the hollows of his cheeks. She quickly went to the kitchen.

Valerian couldn't talk to Jonathan. He ate his cheese and biscuits. After coffee, he said, because he wanted to get out of the dim apartment, 'Let me take you both out for a little. We could go to one of many small museums.'

Jonathan seemed to draw back. 'I think I won't.' He looked at his wife, who was very attentive. 'Perhaps Marion would like to.'

She asked, 'Without you?'

He laughed lightly. 'Valerian won't kill you.'

Everything Valerian said to her sitting beside him in the car as he drove to the museum was shattered by his awareness that he was alone with her; it was as if all his words echoed against her into hundreds of possible reactions, not one of which was clear to him. He could hardly wonder what had happened between her and Jonathan, because even to wonder was perhaps too insistent an inquiry into what was only a sense that something had happened; maybe they themselves were not aware of it, and wouldn't have been able to tell him what it was if he had asked, as Marion wouldn't be able to tell him, if he asked, why she had come with him and remained silent.

The little ceramics museum was converted from a town house. They encountered no one but the uniformed guards.

Valerian took Marion to the top floor first to slowly evolve themselves down to the bottom. There were translucent shades over the large windows, so the light was strained like water pouring into and filling the room; reflections on the glass cases were reflections in the water, and the blue, red, bone-white vases, standing on glass shelves, floated in the aqueous light. Valerian had an image of themselves floating from case to case.

It seemed to him Marion did float off from him, a fraction from the ground, to a case in a far corner. He approached her. He saw her reflection in the glass, and beyond the reflection was a row of vases on a shelf. Their shapes arrested him. Valerian looked from the vases back to Marion; he wondered what she was seeing in them.

She turned away and went to another case, unaware of him. He followed her, examining, after her, the particular vases she had studied, as if to determine what in each one had attracted her enough to stop and stare at it.

They descended to the floor below. In the middle of the room stood a glass case, a crystal cube, and in it, its form multiplied by the six panes of glass, was a single tall vase. Marion stood before it, Valerian behind her. He thought, in the silence, he could hear the vase hum, and the more he looked at it the more it appeared to him that its long contours had nothing to do with clay or glazes; it might, he thought, have been produced by the ringing of a large clear bell, or the striking of a gong, and as the invisible plangent faded, this bright form took shape. Marion remained before it a long time, and Valerian remained behind her.

He could, by refocusing his eyes, see her hair, the side of her face, her shoulders. Neither of them moved. Focusing again on the vase, his eyes were drawn to both their reflections on the glass, and he saw that she had not been looking at the vase, she had been looking at the reflection of him. She immediately shifted her eyes to the vase, but he felt something had been struck by that reflected contact, and it expanded as he had imagined the vase had expanded from one sharp note. He took a step nearer her. His shoulder brushed her, and she turned. She looked up at him for a second, and as she did her eyes, at first bright, went vacant. She smiled. She said, 'I'd like to go.'

'Very well,' he answered.

He stood beside her as she unlocked the door, a heavy door with many small locks. As she opened it, low voices sounded from inside, and she stepped back.

Valerian said, 'Jonathan has visitors.'

She let him go in first.

He found Jonathan alone in the sitting-room listening to the radio. He noticed Marion nevertheless searching the chairs, the divan, the corners, as if she still wasn't certain there was no one else but Jonathan.

Valerian said, 'We thought you were with others.'

Jonathan got up and switched off the radio. 'No,' he said.

The three stood motionless in the dim room. A moment later, Marion turned and left.

Jonathan said, 'I'll walk you back to your place, or do you have your car?'

'No, I've parked it.'

'I'd like a walk.'

Thrust into the light of the street-lamps, bare branches leaning over the park fence cast thin shadows. Jonathan and Valerian walked through them. Valerian described the museum to Jonathan, and Jonathan listened to him for the same reason he had listened to the radio: not because of what was being said, but for the sound, more distinct and placeable than the sounds which had no definite cause but rang out in echoes everywhere. He could not bear the echoes, though his mind, even now with Valerian's voice in his ears, heard them bouncing faintly from the pickets in the fence to a lamp-post, to a stop sign to a closed parked car.

He said, suddenly, to interrupt Valerian, 'I think it was a mistake to stay here.'

There was a long pause from Valerian. 'Then perhaps you should stay away.'

'Perhaps we should go back,' Jonathan said.

'I'm sorry it's been such a disappointment to you.'

'If it is, it isn't as I imagined it might be disappointing. It's not as though nothing has happened.'

Jonathan remarked Valerian's sudden look towards him.

'She's become worse here,' Jonathan continued.

'And you think she'll continue to get worse.'

'I don't know, but I don't want to wait to see.'

'Would you be any more certain of what might happen to her if you went back?'

'No, but there I at least would know where I am.'

Valerian said nothing.

When they reached his door, Jonathan said, 'Do you mind if I come up with you?'

Valerian glanced down at his shoes, and said, looking up again, 'Isn't your wife waiting for you?'

'She'll be all right for a little while.'

Valerian reached to open the door; he held it open for Jonathan to pass through. They climbed the dimly illuminated stairs in silence. It was colder in the stair-well than outside, and colder still – as if the white walls gave off a cold and slightly damp exhalation – inside Valerian's sitting-room. Valerian went to get glasses for drinks, and Jonathan sat, wondering why he had wanted to come up, what he had expected here.

Though they talked, Jonathan was aware of Valerian's preoccupation, as though half his attention were turned towards something too distant for Jonathan to see. Then the talk broke off, and it was as if Valerian's preoccupation broke as well, and he looked at Jonathan as with a slight expression of surprise at seeing him there, but all he said, after a pause, was, 'I wonder if you'd like to see something I bought recently.'

'Yes,' Jonathan said.

He went out and came back holding a small, smooth, grey

globe. He handed it to Jonathan, whose hand dropped slightly under the weight: the globe was made of stone.

Jonathan examined it, then handed it back. He got up. 'I've got to go,' he said. As he was going out the door he turned back and asked, his eyes wide, 'You will continue to come and see Marion, won't you?'

'If you'd like me to.'

'Yes,' Jonathan said.

He walked slowly. Marion, he knew, would be in bed waiting for him.

She lay on her side, her right arm pressed beneath her. She lay very still. She could see nothing but the window, its grey squares blurring into darkness about the edges. She studied them, tried to bring them into focus, as if all she needed to do was to stare hard enough. From the angle at which she was lying, she tried to see other things in the room, but she knew it was only because she could recall where the bureau, a picture, the closet door were and exactly what they looked like that she imagined she could see them now. In fact, she couldn't see a thing, and she closed her eyes, but quickly opened them.

She slowly turned over on her back, as with the stealth of someone who did not want to make noise or be seen moving. Again, she lay still. She was hot. The weight of the blankets was heavy on her chest, stomach, legs. She slid her legs apart. She wondered if she should change position again and lie on her left side, but at the same time she knew there was not one position she had not tried (as if the positions were the combination to a lock which, if she twisted her legs, her arms, her torso, in just the right way, would fly open), there was not one position she could bear to remain in for more than ten deep breaths. She lay flat, and held herself against the compulsion to move. Not only would moving not be a relief, she imagined if she did move someone – perhaps it was only Jonathan – would come into the room and stop her. She knew she couldn't help her imagination which, like her body, could go out of her control; she knew he wasn't there, but she sensed someone, in a corner, behind the closet door, attentive to her. She breathed in and out deeply and felt that her muscles, in rebellion against her drawing them tight, would suddenly jerk free.

She slowly pulled her arms out from beneath the bedclothes and laid them over her head, half clutching her pillow. Her fingers touched the headboard. She lightly tapped at the wood, then scratched it. It extended, flat and blank, beyond her reach. She tapped at it with the backs of her fingers, her finger-nails clicking, her knuckles thudding. She clenched her hands and continued to tap with an increasing and driving impatience that made her tap harder and harder. And then, suddenly, she beat fiercely, and kept beating, so the headboard shook, and the noise was a deep, hollow knocking.

The light came on, a brilliant flash, but she didn't stop. She saw, as if from the deck of a ship rising and falling in a wild sea, the bedclothes surging, then the ceiling light, then the floor, then Jonathan rushing up to her – saw, that is, his feet, his face, his hands reaching towards her. He clutched her wrists. He pressed her arms, stretched over her head, down against the pillow. She tried to pull herself free, wrenching her arms from his grip, but he pressed down harder.

He said, 'Your hands are bleeding.'

At the sound of his voice, she rose up, or the ghost of her rose up, far up, and looked down at the scene of the dishev-elled bed, Jonathan kneeling on the edge and leaning over her, and she, stretched out and writhing, her knuckles skinned and bleeding, staring up, far up, at herself staring down; she saw in her eyes a look that made her stop moving.

'All right,' she said, and her muscles and bones felt as though they unhinged.

Jonathan went into the bathroom and came back quickly with a dripping wet face-cloth with which he wiped her hands. She let him pick up each hand, wipe it, then place it, as if it was an object with no motion of its own, on the top of the blankets, which he smoothed out. She watched him, from that high and disembodied distance, foreshortened, tucking in the blankets, arranging the pillows, combing back her hair with his hands. She saw herself, the sheet folded over the top blanket which lay across her chest, her arms extended and lying on each side of her, her bloody knuckles, as motionless and stark and heavy as if she had suddenly died with her eyes open.

He leaned over her. He asked, 'Do you want anything?'

She didn't respond. She didn't want anything, and he knew she didn't because he knew she never wanted anything.

He said, 'Please answer me, Marion.'

She didn't.

'Please answer me.'

She remained still.

'Shall I come to bed?' he asked, but didn't wait for an answer. He drew back and rapidly undressed, throwing his clothes on the floor. Naked, he ran to shut off the light and returned quickly to bed. She felt the bedclothes rise, and felt his body slide in next to hers. He held her, and she, motionless, sensed her dead weight in his arms. Slowly his arms loosened.

She lay awake as he slept, or pretended to sleep. She felt his breath on her neck, his legs locked about hers, his chest pressed to the side of a breast with a thin film of sweat, his heart.

With a sudden retensing of her muscles, she pulled herself closer to Jonathan and for a convulsive moment she held to him as tightly as she could. He woke.

He said, 'Marion.'

She said, 'Go back to sleep.'

He couldn't sleep. He knew she was awake in his arms, and what she was thinking had nothing to do with either him or her; what she was thinking was as blank as the darkness she visibly projected into the room by her thinking. He thought: she would always leave him out. She moved, pulled out of his arms, and he wondered suddenly why he had ever wanted to be inside. He pressed himself asleep.

The next day, he asked, 'Would you like to see Valerian?'

She didn't react for a moment, then she said, 'Why do you think I should want to see Valerian?'

'He likes you,' Jonathan said.

Marion laughed.

Her laughter made him aware of the hard edges of his bones, his ribs, his skull. He immediately went to the telephone and rang up Valerian at his work. In a loud voice, he asked him to come to dinner that evening. As he spoke, he watched Marion through the doorway of the sitting-room turn her back to him. Jonathan approached her. He said:

'He'll come.'

She said, 'I didn't want to see him.'

'You have no choice now.'

She faced him. 'I didn't want to see him,' she repeated.

'You will see him,' Jonathan said. He stared her down. 'In fact, I think it'll be better if you see him on your own.'

'I won't stay,' she said.

'Yes, you will,' he said. 'I'll make you.'

She walked back and forth.

He said, 'I'd like, now, to be alone.'

'You want me to go out?'

'Yes.'

She put on her heavy coat and left.

He thought, after she was away for an hour, that he should go out and tell her to come back, but he held himself against going. He kept looking out the windows to see if she might be below, in the street or park. The short, cloudy afternoon passed quickly into dusk, then darkness, and twice he put on his coat to go out and twice took it off.

When Valerian came, Jonathan said, 'She's not here. We must go and look for her.'

Valerian's face was suddenly animated as with a great expectancy. He hurried down the stairs before Jonathan. Outside, he waited for Jonathan, and asked, 'How long has she been gone?'

'I don't know,' Jonathan said.

'You were waiting for me to come to help you?'

'Yes.'

Valerian looked away. His breath steamed about him in his excitement. He asked, 'Why did she go?'

'I sent her out. I've been sharp with her. I've had to be. She will only do things if she is forced to.'

'You force her?'

Jonathan said, 'I'll force her till something happens.'

'Oh yes!' Valerian said, and quickly crossed the street, as though something were already happening and he must get to it.

The two men climbed over the park fence, a low picket fence which could not have kept anyone out. Old tramps got in and left empty bottles and newspapers spread out beneath trees, and Valerian sometimes saw, crossing the park in the early morning, a duck, bloody and mutilated, lying in the mud by the pond. He felt the wet ground soft beneath his shoes. He could see nothing but still, shaggy shapes, the trees veins of deeper blackness against the black sky. Standing by Jonathan, both of them unsure which direction they should take, it occurred to him that the park was a country into which they had come illegally and within whose frontier they had stopped.

Jonathan hung back, looking about.

His excitement making him want to go in every direction at once, Valerian touched his elbow. He asked, 'Which way?'

Jonathan hung back a moment longer, then pointed.

They followed a path, just visible in the darkness; it led them beneath bare bushes that branched out over them, and from which drops of water splashed when a branch was snapped by a shoulder or arm or, once, by Valerian's head. The path led to a gazebo set on a small knoll and surrounded by unclipped bushes. Jonathan paused again before it. Valerian passed him and went into the gazebo; its lattice was broken, the thatch of vine hung down through the roof in long dangling garlands. Beneath a wooden bench there was a tramp asleep on newspapers, a ragged overcoat covering him. Valerian could hear him breathe. He left. He whispered to Jonathan:

'That's where you found her last?'

'Yes.'

They went on. The path brought them to a rubbish heap. There was a loud scuttering and sounds of tins hitting one another as they approached. They turned back.

'Where shall we go?' Valerian asked.

Jonathan hunched his shoulders, all at once overcome, it seemed to Valerian, by the enormity of the park. Marion could be anywhere in it.

'Perhaps you should lead,' Jonathan said to him after slowly turning towards all the diverging directions of the path. 'You must know the way better than I do.'

Jonathan was talking in a voice that was perhaps louder than usual – or that now sounded louder than usual – as if he did not care if they were discovered, not only by a guard with a guard dog, but by whatever night-time society inhabited the park.

Valerian, whispering, said, 'Not at night.' But he went ahead.

He could hear Jonathan's steps lagging behind. He didn't want to follow, Valerian thought; he didn't want to find Marion.

Valerian came to a bridge. He stopped at the top of it, and Jonathan came up behind him. Beneath the bridge a stream gurgled into a pond, grey and still, over which they looked. Except for running water and a faint soughing of wind through trees, there was silence, as grey and still, it seemed to Valerian, as the pond. Then Jonathan put his hand on Valerian's shoulder, and, as if this touch produced it, there was a terrible screeching and squawking and splashing of wings beating the water. Valerian jumped away, more, he was aware, from the touch of Jonathan's hand than from the burst of sound.

They continued over the bridge, following the path down a

slope towards the pond's edge, where Valerian saw a figure sitting on a bench.

It was Valerian who drew back this time, Jonathan after him. Valerian could suddenly feel his pulse in all the air about him. Jonathan said, 'There she is.'

'Are you sure?'

'Yes.'

'Shouldn't we go to her?'

Jonathan said nothing. He didn't want to go, obviously, as if, on approaching her, she would turn to them and present them with a face that had undergone a hideous transformation.

Valerian stepped forward, and Jonathan followed. Valerian noticed that she sat bolt upright when she became aware that someone was approaching her, but she didn't turn about to look. She kept her head lowered.

Valerian walked in a wide circle about her to face her. He stood at a distance from her. She raised her head.

He had an abrupt sensation of falling. The sensation made all his thinking and feeling jerk back to some thin edge, but they continued to stare at one another, and then he stepped forward and reached his hand out, and it was as if, finally, he jumped, jumped into the width and breadth of what he saw in her face, from which he knew he would never now be capable of pulling himself back. He loved her, he saw, with the inevitability and force of a body dropping from a great height.

Jonathan, further away from Marion than he, watched him lean towards her. He could not be sure if Valerian was reaching his hand to her or if, two fingers extended, he was pointing to some point in mid-air half way between them at which they both stared, but he was suddenly sure, as if the point were the centre in a complex and symmetrical diagram of the conjunction of their momentarily poised bodies, that something was fixed between them, and that it left him out. He, too, simply stared.

Then Marion lowered her head.

Jonathan heard Valerian say, 'It's cold. We should go back.'
The two of them might have simply taken a walk together,
stopped here by the pond briefly, and now Valerian thought it
was time to return to the warmth.

She didn't take his hand, but she got up. She followed directly behind him, so Jonathan could not see her until Valerian
came up to him and stepped aside, but the moment she found
herself facing her husband she turned away. She stood still. She
was trembling. Jonathan watched Valerian step around to face
her, to look at her and say, 'Come on, Marion.' He wondered
where he meant to take her.

In file, Jonathan first, Valerian last, Marion between, they
slowly walked to the fence. Valerian took off his overcoat and
spread it over the top of the pickets to pad them so Marion
could sit when he hoisted her up and Jonathan, having jumped
to the other side, grabbed her to balance her. She swung her
legs over, and Jonathan helped her down to the sidewalk. Valerian jumped over, took up his overcoat, and the three of them
crossed the street.

As they approached the entrance to the mansion block, Jonathan pulled against their all going in together. At the door, he
stopped and asked Valerian :

'Do you mind going up with Marion? I must take a little
walk.'

'No, of course not,' Valerian said. He pushed the door open
for Marion to pass through.

Jonathan walked around the block. His legs felt weak. He
turned a corner into a side street, narrow and paper-littered,
where rubbish fires were smouldering in the gutters. He
walked down the middle of the street, and thought : he could
not have gone up to that little flat with them, could not have
listened to them speak, or, worse, not speak. He turned another corner. He suddenly imagined the street wide and open
before him, as though he had just come out of a large dark
house, the recollection of which repulsed him, and, leaving
them inside, had closed the door after him, and he was, even

walking down the dim and littered street, walking far away from them.

The next day, he and Valerian retraced their steps from the bench where they had found Marion to look for a thin gold bracelet which she had dropped from her wrist, though he suspected she had thrown it into the pond. They searched through the grass, shook the bushes.

'We won't find it,' Jonathan said.

He didn't care. It was Valerian who had insisted on looking when Marion, the night before, had said, just as Valerian was leaving, as though it were a farewell remark, 'My bracelet is gone.'

'It is gone,' Jonathan said.

But Valerian kept searching through the branches of an evergreen bush.

'There's no point looking,' Jonathan said. 'In any case, she wouldn't care even if we did find it.'

Valerian paid no attention to him. He kicked over a heap of rotten leaves.

'Leave it.'

'Let me look through this.'

'Leave it.'

Jonathan made his voice sharp. Valerian turned to look at him.

'You don't want to find it,' Valerian said flatly.

'No,' Jonathan said, 'I don't.'

'Why?'

'Because it's of no interest to me.'

Their breath steamed in the cold damp air.

'Didn't you give it to her?' Valerian asked.

'Yes.'

'I don't believe you're not interested.'

'You don't?' Jonathan smiled. 'Perhaps you don't believe it's possible for anyone to be any less interested than you.'

Valerian said nothing for a moment, then asked, quietly, 'Is it so obvious?'

'Yes.' Jonathan smiled more broadly. 'But that doesn't matter either. I'll be leaving.'

He could see a slight panic come into Valerian's eyes, startling in his otherwise impassive face.

'You'll leave her?' Valerian asked.

'Yes.'

Valerian was holding a bunch of broken weeds; he dropped them and rubbed his hands together. 'You'll leave her helpless?'

'I can't do anything. I know that.'

'She can't be helped?'

'I can't help her.'

Valerian looked down at his hands, which he slowly kept rubbing together. He looked up at Jonathan and squinted as though there were a strong light in his eyes. 'You're leaving her to me, is that it?'

Jonathan shook his head. 'I'm not leaving her to anyone or anything. She'll have to get on by herself. I'll give her as much money as I can, so she will not be dependent on anyone for that. She'll be free, she'll have all the room in the world. You don't ever have to see her again.'

Valerian continued squinting as against a painful glare.

As Jonathan packed, Marion sat on the edge of the bed and watched him. He pulled out drawer after drawer of the bureau and placed his socks, shirts, underwear into the suitcase, spread out open on the bed beside her. Her eyes followed him from the bureau to the bed, back and forth, which made him so conscious of his movements he had to tell himself exactly what to do: pick up a pile of handkerchiefs, place them in a corner of the suitcase. He went to the wardrobe and took out a handful of ties; he stood for a moment, the ties dangling from his hand, not quite sure what he should do with them. He glanced at Marion, who had been staring at him, and when their eyes met she lowered her head.

Her lowered head exposed her nape, and the sight of it made Jonathan drop his arm, so the ties trailed on the floor;

but a moment later he jerked his arm up and threw the ties, which slithered, into the suitcase.

She raised her head. Her eyes swept past him as she looked around the room.

He held a pair of shoes. They were scuffed and stuck about the rims with dry mud; he had been wearing them the time he went into the park with Valerian to find her. He turned them over and looked at the soles, caked with more dry mud and crushed grass. He held out the shoes to her and said, 'I think you'd better clean these.'

She stared at them as if they were floating by themselves in the air before her. He thrust them closer to her face. She blinked a number of times, and he thought she was going to refuse. Then she reached out for them.

'You know where the polish and rags are,' he said.

'Yes,' she said. She placed the shoes on the floor, went out and came back with a box. She again sat on the bed, took out the polish and rags and, resting one of the shoes on her lap, began to smear the polish over it.

'You'll get yourself covered with polish,' he said.

'It doesn't matter,' she answered.

No, of course not, he thought. He turned away from her, went to the window and looked down at the park, where a misty rain made the green lawns and bare brown-grey trees appear to expand into mist themselves. A man wearing a bright yellow slicker rode a bicycle along a path. He heard a shoe thump to the floor. He didn't move, but continued to look out. When the second one, thrown with a louder thump, fell, he turned around, went and picked them up, wrapped them in paper and stuffed them into the case. Marion's lap was littered with dry clods, some of which had smashed into loose earth.

Jonathan said. 'Hold down the case while I snap it shut.'

She did as she was told. She sat on it.

He stood back.

'Did you put in your things from the bathroom?' she asked.

'Yes.'

She stood on the other side of the bed. He narrowed his eyes. He thought: she would accommodate herself to his going, as she had accommodated herself to his being there, as she had accommodated herself to the blankness which she saw in everything, the blankness about which and beyond which there was nothing to say, which was, reduced to its essential, herself stretched out and exposed on a slab.

His bag was heavy. He opened the door to the flat, stepped out, then stopped. She was standing behind his back, just inside the door. His bag pulled at his arm and shoulder. He faced her. Her eyes were large, her irises flat and trembling discs, and she didn't blink. He could not imagine what she was looking at. He placed his bag down. She put her hand on the door, and he wondered if she were about to close it or if she were supporting herself. He said:

'Valerian –'

He saw nothing in her face. She didn't move. He had to make himself turn and walk away.

In the taxi, he wondered if the best he could have done for Marion would have been, not just to leave her, but to leave her unprovided for, to leave her without money or a lease in her name. If she *had* to work, if her life were determined by that necessity –

The thought broke into his reasoning that she would have not thought her life worth working for. He thought of her, now alone. With a finger he made circles in the mist of the little side window.

He had refused to let himself make a sign to her that he was upset that he was going, as he knew that she, as aware of his going as he, more aware because it left her cut off from everything she had known, refused to let herself consider it was anything to be upset about. She wouldn't be upset. And yet, he knew that in the whole course of their relationship she had been waiting for something to occur which would upset her, which she could not, finally, bear. This final gesture, his going, was not enough, because she knew he was going away because

54

of her, and nothing that had to do with her gave her reason to do anything but bear it. He knew she despised herself to that extent: she believed that whatever she herself thought or felt, whatever she herself caused, was so without necessity that she must ignore it all, must deny, deny anything in her that did not have to do with sleeping, eating, shitting. She waited for what she could not deny, for what would force her – literally force her, as a child rigid in its obstinacy had to be forced – to act, to shout. But nothing had forced her; he, Jonathan, had tried, but he did not have the determination and strength; she was stronger than he, stronger in her denying than he was in forcing, even when the forcing was cruel, for if he was cruel to her, she took that in, too, as something she somehow deserved – everything she could bear, everything that tested her acceptance but didn't overwhelm it, she deserved. He had never been able to test her; even at his cruellest, he had never been a block to her. He hadn't known how to be, didn't want to be. But that was what she wanted: something which held against her, which she would never be able to break.

He imagined her now wandering from room to room. He saw her pick up things – a book, a coffee cup, the telephone receiver – and put them down. She would go into the bedroom and open and shut all the drawers of his bureau, open and close the doors of his wardrobe. She would go out and into the sitting-room, sit on a sofa, get up, walk to a picture of the sea which hung a little askew and study it. Below it was a table, and on the table was a porcelain pot. She would pick it up; all her muscles convulsing about her desire to smash it, she would hold it and stare at it.

He wondered how soon after he left would Valerian go to her.

Ronald Ghee held the door open. Valerian stood outside.

Valerian said, 'I'm sorry I didn't phone before coming.'

'You know you don't have to do that,' Ronald answered.

Valerian looked past him into the flat. 'Is there someone there?'

Ronald smiled. He opened the door wider and Valerian came in. 'You see, I'm alone,' he said.

Valerian took off his coat and threw it on a chair.

'I can't recall the last time you were here,' Ronald said.

'Don't reproach me for it.'

Ronald turned away. 'No, no.'

The two men stood in the centre of the room.

'I thought you might have gone away,' Ronald said.

'I've been around.'

'Oh.' Ronald paused. 'And what have you been doing?'

'I saw a lot of Jonathan Rack and his wife.'

'You no longer do?'

'Jonathan has left,' Valerian said.

'I see,' Ronald said. After a moment, he asked, 'Why did you come to see me now?'

Valerian hunched his shoulders. 'I don't know,' he said. He sat.

Ronald stood over him. 'I'd ask you to get out if I really believed you were intentionally treating me so flatly.'

Valerian looked up at him. He said, 'I'm sorry.'

Ronald again asked, 'Why did you come?'

Valerian said nothing.

Ronald, too, sat. He held his chin in his hand and waited. He said, 'Because Rack left?'

Valerian said, 'Oh, he can take care of himself; his wife –'

'Should you mind about her?'

'No, there's no reason in the world why I should, but I do.'

'No doubt it's better for him that he did go.'

'For him, yes, but not for her.'

'Because she's alone?'

'Completely.'

Ronald took his hand away from his chin. 'Except for you?'

'I shouldn't imagine that makes much difference to her.'

'Then she prefers to be alone.'

'Perhaps. I don't know. She's not well. It's impossible to know what she prefers.'

'I'd take her for her word,' Ronald said. 'I'd leave her alone.'

'For her sake?'

'For yours. She's not well. Stay away from her.'

Valerian said nothing.

Ronald spoke quickly. 'She doesn't have anything to do with you, with your friends, with your work or world. You know she doesn't.'

'But if she's not well, I can't just leave her.'

'You're making excuses. She doesn't *want* you.'

'No,' Valerian said. 'But I want her.' He looked at Ronald. 'You see, everything in me has changed. I want her.'

There was silence.

'I want her more than you can imagine,' Valerian said.

'I can imagine,' Ronald said after a moment. He added, 'But if you know that, why come to me as though to get me to condone it?'

'Condone it, no. I wanted you to tell me to stay away from her.'

'Haven't I?' Ronald got up, and Valerian did also, and stood near him. 'But I understand wanting,' Ronald said.

He had hardly said it when, with a sound that might have been a moan, Valerian put his hands on Ronald's shoulders and pulled at him so that their jaws cracked together, and Ronald felt that he was pulling him down; then Valerian let go and pulled away.

Ronald said, 'You know, you haven't changed, nothing has; or if anything has, it's only that you are more heavily and insupportably serious than you were. You won't have changed until you make up your mind that none of this matters.'

'How can I make up my mind about something over which I have no control?'

'You really are helpless?'

Valerian turned around to him. Ronald grabbed him by the upper arm. He could feel the muscle.

He said, 'Then you'd better go to her.'

'Now?'

'Right now. Ring her up, don't ring her up, that's up to you. But you'd better go.'

He wanted Valerian to get out of his flat.

Valerian hurried. He was not sure why or for what, but the idea pressed on him that he was too late. He imagined her, alone, in a dark room.

She had been sitting for a long time in the room. She didn't know how long Jonathan had been gone. It had been light when he left, and now it was dark.

She thought: when someone left, it was very difficult to see him in another place, sitting, standing, walking about, in a certain chair, room, building; he was simply gone, and was no longer, for her, a body, but had become like the darkness, an absence, and it was as impossible to think about the absence as it was impossible to think about the darkness – there it was, around her, now empty, still, and she in it was empty and still, herself as bodily absent from the room as Jonathan was.

She wondered if this was what one felt when a person close to one died. There was nothing she could think about the person, because there was nothing left to which she could fix her mind. Everything about him became darkness, and all she must do was keep the darkness still.

But that required a concentration that cut back, cut and cut away, everything that moved, everything that rose up in confusion: stars, sky, earth, elements, plants, cabbages, leeks, animals, insects, calves, serpents, fever, plague, war, famine, vice, adultery, incest – None of these mattered, none of these, she insisted; what mattered was to be still, to be calm.

Jonathan was gone, had himself cut himself away from her. She wouldn't allow herself to think about him.

She listened. She heard a low sound.

And if she cut herself away from herself, she thought, what

would that matter? It wouldn't matter, not only because there was no one around her to whom cutting herself away would make any difference, but because there was nothing about her the loss of which would make a difference to herself; dying would not make a difference.

She got up and went into the bedroom, where she lit the light and saw herself in the mirror above the bureau. She touched her face.

She thought: if she could want nothing more than to sleep and eat and shit, she would be calm, because she would have everything.

She saw, in the mirror, her eyes. She looked away.

But she wanted more, and to have it she couldn't die, because dying would make this one unthinkable difference: dead she would not be aware that she was, and the awareness that she was she could only have here, in this room. She had to continue sleeping, eating, shitting for that awareness.

She must make the awareness everything: a darkness so great nothing survived in it. She must have it, because nothing else mattered. Against the awareness of darkness, not even her dying, really dying, mattered.

She lay on the bed. Her mind, momentarily passing beyond its own thinking, went blank, and emerging from the blackness the first thing she noted was the low sound.

She held herself still, while knowing that she would not, in a moment, be able to hold herself still any longer, that the stillness was only a thin idea she did not have the strength to realize.

It came over her, a physical apprehension, that if she moved she would start up what was held in check by her remaining still. Against this stillness, something was, was always, building up about her; her rigidity gave way to a fluttering spasm through her legs.

The sudden ringing of the doorbell sent another spasm through her. She lay trying to recall where she was. The bell rang again, and she thought: Jonathan had come back.

She did not know if she should answer the door. She wasn't able to make a decision. She rose from the bed, and went into the hall.

Valerian came in as though he had come in an emergency. She hardly said anything to him. She showed him into the sitting-room as if to a sick-room. She didn't know what to say. He was flushed. He had obviously hurried, and though he now saw there was no reason for his having hurried the state of emergency seemed to continue in his restlessness. She sat and he walked about the room saying, 'It was cold today. It is –'

She watched him. He stopped in the middle of the room, facing her. As if his body had been, since he came in, hoisted on a rack that now broke down, his shoulders dropped, his arms hung loose, his body appeared to be suddenly without support. He said, 'I wanted to see you.' He sat across from her, and she rose.

She went to the window to look out, though all she could see was darkness.

After a while, she heard him rise also and, it seemed, step towards her. A feeling came over her that he would come near and reach out and touch her, and a little shock of fear passed across her chest. But he didn't come near. She wasn't able to tell where in the room he was. She could hardly keep herself from turning to see, because she imagined that wherever he was, and whatever he was doing, he was waiting for her to turn to him. She touched the glass with the tips of her fingers, and with the slight shock of the cold there came to her a sharp sense of what he might be doing, or waiting to do: he was waiting for her to turn so he could make some sign, which he was now silently considering, that would immediately mitigate all her tense reserve.

Looking at the misty window, she said, 'It's strange that when someone leaves, especially to go far, it's very difficult to place in your mind where he's gone. He's simply gone, and there's nothing more, really, you can know than that.'

'You mean Jonathan?' Valerian asked.

60

She could not tell from his voice where he was in the room; his voice made the little flash of fear pass through her from armpit to armpit.

'Yes.'

She said, suddenly, 'You know, he was always expecting me to change.'

She turned to Valerian.

Valerian smiled. It took her a moment to take the smile in, but when she did she realized it was as if he had all at once stripped her, and her reaction was as if to clutch something and, if he took one step nearer her, to thrust it at him.

He continued to smile. A prickling ran over her skull and down her shoulder blades. She knew nothing about Valerian; as openly unprotected as she was, she might be facing someone who would step towards her and press her hard against the window until it shattered and she would be pushed out. Again, an intense prickling ran across her skull and down her back, and her skin became tight. The moments passed slowly, but something remained in the room, something that projected from him like an emanation, and she knew, of course, what he wanted : not to murder her, no – though she imagined the effect would somehow be no less violent and, for him, no less considered – but to approach her to touch her.

She quickly turned around to the window and, hooking her fingers under the sash lifts, opened it. The dark outside cold blasted over her. She leaned out a little. She breathed deeply and closed her eyes. When she felt a hand on her shoulder, she didn't move.

Valerian said, 'You'll fall.'

He closed the window.

As he left, she said, 'You shouldn't come here.'

He asked, 'Will you stop me if I do?'

She didn't know what to answer. 'You shouldn't,' she said.

He smiled.

He left, but after, it seemed to her that he had forgotten something in the flat, and that he would be back to take it. She looked around the sitting-room. She found nothing.

He fell asleep with the radio, turned low, beside his bed. When he woke, the station had closed down for the night, and there came, with wavering static, broadcasts from very far away, some in unknown languages, the minuscule voices rising and sinking away.

He thought of Ronald on one side of him. He thought of Marion on the other. He thought of them standing far enough from him that to speak to one of them he had to move either to the right or the left, away from one towards the one he would speak to, leaving one isolated − isolated, that is, from him, and when he turned back he might perhaps find the one he had momentarily left gone. Now, he stood equidistant from them, and kept them at his right and left, but if he stepped left towards Marion then turned back to his right he would see that Ronald was no longer there; if he lost Ronald he would lose everything that was familiar to him.

But he longed for Marion, and his longing swelled out with all the darkness of the risk in it.

Valerian saw Ronald step into the room and stop, suddenly seeing, by a window, Marion Rack. He knew that Ronald had thought he would be alone with him; he went to stand by Marion. Ronald approached them. Marion held out a hand a little way from her waist. Ronald didn't reach for it.

He said, 'I thought Valerian wouldn't bring us together.'

'Why shouldn't he?' she asked.

'To keep us apart, as he kept me apart from your husband,' Ronald said. 'He didn't tell me you were going to be here.' He didn't look at Valerian.

'Perhaps he thought you wouldn't come if you knew,' she said.

'I wanted you to see one another,' Valerian said, his voice low.

They sat at a round table, the two men at equidistant curves from Marion.

Ronald could see Valerian's head, minute, reflected in each

of Marion's eyes. He was saying to Valerian:

'Because I think you should go away. I think you need a change.'

'Where should I go?'

'I could recommend a place.'

'Where?'

'An island, bleak and far.'

'How appealing you make it sound!'

'I'm not being ironic. It's just what you need. I'd go with you.'

Valerian looked at Marion. He said, 'Maybe we could all go.'

Marion said nothing.

Ronald said, 'I would go to be alone.'

'You wouldn't be alone if I were with you,' Valerian said.

Ronald smiled. 'Oh, you –'

Valerian smiled back; he didn't say, no, he wouldn't go away with Ronald, he simply looked at him. The smiles of the two men seemed to rise up and meet, to hang suspended over the table, a point of reference to everything they shared which Marion knew nothing about. She didn't want to know. She wondered why she was with them.

She said, 'I must go.'

Valerian's eyes jumped to her. 'Please stay,' he said.

Marion got up. 'Don't come with me.'

Valerian stood.

When she left, Ronald asked, 'Why did you bring us together?'

Valerian's face was without expression. 'I hoped you'd get along.'

'We don't. We couldn't.'

Valerian looked away. 'No, perhaps not.' After a moment, he asked, 'Why do you think you can't get along with her?'

'I don't think anything of her. Of you in relation to her, I think you're seeing things that aren't there, are hearing vibrations where there're no sounds at all.'

Valerian walked the long windy way back to his flat.

Marion heard the owls in the park from her bedroom. Their cries seemed to be part of the wet wind that blew through the cracks of the badly fitted windows. She imagined the wind had passed through a great space, and continued through a great space.

Whatever Valerian wanted from her, she thought, he would not get it. All he could do was draw on her, as blank as she was, the circles and squares of what he projected on to her; if he thought he could get anything from her, it was only because he himself put it there first. She must let him know this before his circles and squares became to him a confused tangle of lines, and he would be caught in them, and would try to catch her in them.

The only way to let him know that, she thought, was to simply cut herself away from him, to cut away from him any sense he might have had that he could see anything in her; he saw nothing in her.

Valerian talked. He talked, it seemed to her, in a wide-reaching attempt to strike what she might respond to, as if he were searching about for a shape she might recognize, or a combination of sounds that would suddenly involve her like music. She noted that he did not mention his friend. Daffodils, crushed together in a vase on the coffee table, gave a slight, humid scent to the air – hardly a scent at all, she thought, but a damp warmth about her nose and mouth as they slowly wilted. Valerian drew one out. He held the stem in one hand and the blossom in the open palm of his other hand.

He said, 'There's no point in going away, in going back. You won't live with Jonathan. You yourself said it wouldn't do either of you any good.'

'I wouldn't be going for Jonathan,' she said.

'Then why? There's really no reason for you to be there rather than here.'

'There's no reason for me to be here.'

He said, 'There are reasons.'

64

She tried to look at him. 'None that I can see,' she said after a moment.

'I can show you,' he said.

She said, 'And if I denied what you showed me?'

'You couldn't deny it.'

'There's nothing I can't deny,' she said.

He smiled. 'That you'll die?'

'That's in itself a denial,' she said.

'Is it? How can you know, as you can't know anything about it?'

She said nothing.

'Take the flower,' he said.

'No,' she said.

He held the daffodil closer to her. 'Take it.'

She turned her head away.

'Take it.'

She remained rigid.

'You're frightened,' he said.

'I'm not frightened of anything,' she said; 'I'm not interested.'

'You're frightened of staying here.'

She pulled the flower from his hand and shoved it among the others in the vase.

She noted a flush come to his cheeks and forehead. He didn't seem to know what to do or where to move to. In three strides, he came around the coffee table and and sat beside her on the sofa. The cushions sank towards him. She inclined away. After a moment, he leaned forward and picked up a pen from the table, stared at it, then threw it down.

'If you have to have a reason for staying, why can't it be, simply, that you don't know, can't know, what may happen if you did stay?'

'That's just taking a risk.'

'Well, then, risk choosing to stay. Risk taking up anything from the table – the flower, the pen, anything – and saying: I'm going to stay because of this.'

She looked down at the jumble of things on the table: a spoon, a nutcracker, a bowl of walnuts, a large button, an empty cup, an orange. Her hands were lying palms upward, the fingers slightly curled, as if she were holding invisible objects. Valerian reached across and put a hand in one of hers. She didn't pull her hand away – she didn't, she knew, because she would not want him to think she was frightened of him.

'You won't take the risk?' he asked quietly, their bodies motionless, both aware that the slightest jolting movement on either part might set into uncontrollable action gestures which, at this still moment, neither could be sure might not end up in a sudden struggle.

She drew her hand away. She rose.

She said, 'Do you imagine when I say I must go away, that I'm going because of you?'

'Yes,' he said.

'No.' she answered. 'It has nothing to do with anyone, with anything.'

He rose too.

'If you listened to me,' he said. 'If you gave me a chance.'

She smiled, a thin line. 'To do what?'

He didn't know what to say. The smile went from her face, and in its place he saw a hard blankness sharpen the planes of her cheeks, forehead, jaw. There was nothing he could say, he knew, that would make a difference to her.

'You won't let me try to show you –'

She cut him off. 'Your friend was right: you should go away.'

'As you will?'

'Yes.'

Staring at him, she saw the pupils of his eyes pulsing, as though he were, with their tiny indrawing contractions, trying to take her in bodily; she kept looking at his eyes.

When she caught herself looking, it occurred to her how very aware she was of him standing before her, as if his clothes were skin, were a part of a sudden nudity that had arrested all her thinking. She found herself studying the soft weave of his sweater, the open collar about his neck. She quickly turned away.

'You'd better go.'

'No,' he said.

'You'd better.'

'No,' he said.

'What do you think you'll get if you stay?'

His jaw was set.

'You won't get anything,' she said. 'Even if you stayed here for ever, you wouldn't get anything.'

'I will stay for ever,' he said.

'You will.'

'Yes.'

She turned away and walked across the room to go out, but stopped, her back to him, at the door. She turned round. He was lying, like a corpse, on the floor.

She went out. She went to her bedroom and closed the door after her. She sat on her bed. She did not know what was happening.

A long time passed. She didn't move. She decided: nothing was happening. She undressed and got into bed.

But she kept listening for a sound of him moving, of the door to the flat closing behind him. She heard nothing. Her awareness of him in the other room kept her wide awake, and she sensed the awareness circle above her body lying in the bed.

She pressed her fingers across her breasts, then pressed them into her thighs and pushed slightly. Her flesh seemed to her to have a thin space beneath it filled with a heavy liquid, so it floated and would, if she pressed too hard, slip. She pressed deeply into her hips, her stomach, her abdomen. When she placed one hand flat against the base of her throat and pressed upward, she felt the skin pulling against her breasts. She ran her hands over her body, and as she did her hands seemed to become immense, and her body beneath them became immense too. She could almost feel the pores at her fingertips, and the pubic hairs she encountered were gigantic.

She broke out into a slight, hot sweat which she knew would quickly turn cold if she didn't do what she could to keep it warm, to keep up the flushes of her immense body.

If he were there now, she thought, if Valerian were there, she would expose herself in a way that wouldn't leave one narrow corner concealed, that would leave her as flat and open as an uncovered mattress. She exposed her skin, her nipples, the tip of her clitoris, as if for his examination. She arched her back, she spread open her legs for him. She would, if she could, draw off her skin, exposing her muscles, her veins, her lungs and stomach and intestines and heart, exposing every narrow crease in her body, every crevice and fold of fat inside her, exposing it all to the certain knowledge that there was nothing more to her passion than her starkness.

With the pre-dawn, she was awake, her mind wide with his presence in the flat.

She put on a robe. She went into the sitting-room. The lights were on, pale in the rising light from outside, the room was as she left it, and Valerian was lying on the floor, his eyes closed. As she slowly approached him everything in her drew away from him, so it was as if she were moving forward and back at once. He suddenly opened his eyes, but stared up straight.

Above him, she asked, 'What do you want? What do you want from me?'

Without moving his head he shifted his eyes slightly to look at her.

'Please get up,' she said.

He got up.

'Please leave me alone. Please do that.'

He left.

She sat. She thought: she mustn't see him, she mustn't. She looked about the room which appeared to fill with harsh white light; she had to shade her eyes.

Each time the telephone rang her alarm at still being where

she was, at not having left, made her try to decide quickly where she would go, and how. She never answered the telephone. When it stopped, and over the long silent periods, it came to her that going meant to go to another place, and she couldn't think of herself in another place; she could only think of herself going, of no longer being where she was. Then, after days, the doorbell began to ring, again and again, at different hours, so she sometimes thought it rang when it didn't, as though the echoes were in her head, and her alarm made her want to get out of the flat as soon as possible, even if she left everything behind. The sound of ringing ceased to have anything to do with the bell. She wouldn't answer. She hoped he would think she had gone. He persisted. She tried, finally, to pack; she packed one suitcase, closed it, and looking at it wondered where she would go. She went out for walks, to the library, to the park.

Beside the bench on which she sat was a large wet bush, which many little invisible birds, darting from twig to twig, shook; they chirped, high, clear, and she imagined for a moment that the shaken bush was itself emitting song.

In her restlessness, she tried to concentrate on the singing. Across the lawn before her was another bench, and on the bench a man was sitting. A woman wheeled a baby carriage across the lawn. She thought: what would she do? What?

Valerian wondered, after so much silence, if he should break in.

He held his finger on the bell. She didn't answer. He came away from her door and descended the long flights to the outside. He went into the park.

He saw her sitting on a bench across a lawn. A man was next to her. Valerian was not sure if they were talking. He stood in full view of her.

She didn't see him, or made no sign that she did. After a while she got up, and the man got up beside her. She walked ahead of the man, leading him along a path, out through the gate, across the street, and into her building. Valerian stood where he was, looking at the building as if he could see them both climbing the stairs, could see Marion opening the door with a key, could see them step into her flat, the man taking off his coat as he turned to her.

He was sure, as certainly as if he could see them, that, in the suspended space of her room, they were making love. It would be a kind of love-making that was meant, not to bring the man, to bring any man, close to her, but to distance him; she would project the image of herself and the man on to the wall, and stare at it, in the same way he, now, stared at the image projected on the brick façade, on the trees, on the window of what must have been her bedroom.

He thought: he was a fool. He repeated it over and over, and with the tempo of his repetition there came over him a kind of sexual hysteria, as deep and as insistent as his self-reproach. Ronald Ghee was right; what he was right about Valerian, now, was too excited to be sure; he simply was, in what he was, right, and it was Ronald's reproachful rightness which made Valerian see himself somehow getting into the flat, grabbing the man from Marion, and, to show her at what distance a man could be put, beating him, beating him till he succumbed to a sexual assault so impersonal the man would not even know if it was human. He hated that man.

Not her, not her.

He waited. He moved to the fence and leaning on it stared at the windows, at the entrance.

From her window, Marion saw him below leaning on the park fence. She herself leaned against the window jamb so he could not see her and continued to look down at him. She felt as though she had just escaped drowning, and was so weak she wondered if she was sorry she had escaped. She thought: and did Valerian suppose he was watching, guarding her, in case she did drown? What did he want from her that he could not get, much more simply, from any other woman? He was staring right up at the window. She drew back. She watched him turn away, his arms crossed. When he turned back to look up again, she suddenly, impulsively, stood near the window. He saw her. He walked the length of the fence to the gate, crossed the street, and disappeared below her through the entrance.

He didn't ring, he knocked. He knocked so she thought he would crack his knuckles.

Outside her door, he knocked and heard the echoes of his knocks down the empty stair-well.

When the door suddenly gave way, he was frightened. She was standing before him. Her face looked as though it had been held underwater for a long period: her lips and cheeks appeared swollen, her eyes were in slits. She asked, her voice hoarse:

'What do you want?'

'I want to see you.'

'You see me.'

'I want to come in.'

'No.'

'Because someone else is in there?'

'There's no one else in here.'

'I saw you come up with someone.'

'I know you saw me.'

'You were aware I was watching you?'

'Yes. But there's no one here now.'

'Who was he?'

'I don't know. I don't know and don't care.'

'And you brought him here.'

'Yes,' she said, 'yes, yes, I brought him here.'

He paused. 'Would you have if I hadn't been standing there to see? Would you have?'

Her face twisted up in pain. 'Go away,' she said, 'go away.' She closed the door.

He knocked, wildly. She opened the door a little. Tears were running down her face.

She said, 'Valerian, please – '

Valerian pushed his way in. Once inside, near her, he had no idea what to say or do. He thought: there was something he wanted to show her, which was why he had come, but how could he show her anything when all he knew of what he wanted to show her was a wild sense he himself could not grasp.

He could only think to say, 'You must go out. I'll take you out. We must get out.'

Tears continued to run down her face. 'Now?'

'Yes.'

'I can't.'

'Yes, now,' he said.

'I can't, I can't.'

He picked up her coat from a chair in the hall and held it open for her to put her arms into the sleeves. She put her arms through.

They walked along a sheep path across fields on which snow lay in melting patches. Above them, the clouds, low, flat, grey and wet, spread out like more snow patches.

Marion followed Valerian. In the distance was a long line of firs. The light was behind them; it was only when she reached them that she was able to see, beyond the dark trunks and drooping branches, a grey-green hill. Valerian led her towards the hill.

As they climbed, passing from gorse to scrub to bunches of dry grass among stones and crusted snow, she felt that he was taking her to a place he had decided on beforehand; he walked as though he knew exactly where he was going. It was cold; up high, the wind blew. He helped her up the side of a crumbling ledge. She wouldn't ask him where they were going. She simply followed. He remained silent.

They stopped at the top of the hill. She saw, on the other side, a long valley down which the light, like a river, was flowing. She turned to Valerian, who was looking out over the valley. Waiting for him to move, she studied him. He turned to her, and she turned away.

They descended into the valley. At the bottom of the hill

there was a pine wood, all the trees, their high thin trunks bare and smooth, in rows. The path led inside. Entering was like entering a structure of long narrow corridors. Inside, the stillness was deep and damp-warm, and the only immediate sound was the sound of dripping water; then, as over a long distance, she heard the wind swishing the branches at the top of the woods. They stopped.

She said, 'I think I've been here before.'

'You came with Jonathan?'

'No. I couldn't have. I never came to the country with Jonathan.'

He blinked rapidly as he looked at her. Behind him was a long corridor of trees, and at right-angles on either side of him were dark corridors, high and narrow. 'How could you have been here?'

She shook her head and shoulders as though she were trying to shake off what she said at the same time. 'I don't know.'

He raised his gloved hands, palms outward. It happened often enough now for her to expect it, but, with each instance, it alarmed her for a flashing second : she thought, now, he was going to push her violently against a tree. He reached out and held her by her upper arms. He drew her closer, and her body went loose; he was holding her up. He held her away from him, but close enough so his eyes appeared huge, and she saw in them that he was possessed, and if she didn't go away, didn't break away as quickly as possible, she would not be able to go at all because he would stop her. She felt very cold. His breath steamed into her face. She pulled away. He released her. She went to lean against a tree.

He left her. He walked among the trees, out of sight. Water dripped about her, and high above, unseen, the branches swished.

She went to find him. The bracken tangled about her ankles. The fir trees, straight, followed close on one another, and between them she saw the dun floor of the woods stretching in all directions. She hurried.

The woods ended abruptly. She stood before a stone wall, on the other side a field. Sheep grazed. They raised their heads in her direction when she climbed up on to the stone wall. Across the field was Valerian. She didn't know what he was doing. As she climbed down, a stone rolled out of the wall. The sheep suddenly turned and ran; each one had a red stain on its shaggy coat.

When she got to him, she touched his elbow. He swung around to her. His bright clean cheeks and forehead, his eyes, his hair, his ears red from the cold, struck her suddenly as belonging to a man she had just then met, and she felt spring up in her a sensation that rose out of her to meet him with a smile. It lasted only a second. When he smiled back, the sensation was cut off, but he had caught enough of it, she saw, to try to retain it; he kept smiling, and said:

'You're not hopeless, you know.'

She smiled again, but it was a different kind of smile. 'You know that, do you?' she said.

'Yes,' he answered.

He took off a glove and touched her neck with the tips of his fingers.

It got dark as they drove back. She sat, silent and motionless, beside him, as though she did not want to remind him that she was there. She thought: she'd quickly leave him, would jump out of the car and slam the door before he had a chance to shut off the ignition. But instead of stopping at her entrance he drove past it. She raised a hand to indicate that they had gone too far. He stopped before the entrance to his building.

She said, 'I must go home.'

'Come up with me,' he said.

'I must go back.'

'I want to show you something,' he said.

She went.

She climbed the stairs behind him. The stair-well was almost dark. She grasped the rail.

She held back when he opened the door. He drew her in by her arm.

Inside, she stood back from him. He lit the light. She tried to look at him. 'What is it?' she asked.

'What I wanted to show you?'

She didn't have time to answer. He took her in his arms.

She let her body go dead, and he let her go, but he held her hand. He brought the hand to his lips. When he licked her palm, he felt her arm jerk back, as if he had stuck a pin in it. She was staring straight at him, and there was nothing in her eyes. Shaken, he smiled, but there was still no expression. A sweeping surge came over him to make her react. He raised her hand again and bit the soft pad beneath her thumb. He bit it so he could feel the edges of his teeth close together. He grabbed her wrist. He would force her to react, he thought, but for a second his mind detached itself from itself and he saw himself from her point of view, ridiculously sucking at her hand.

A second later he felt her fingers close over his face, felt them moving over his forehead, nose, cheek. He clutched her wrist in both his hands. He closed his eyes. He felt her fingertips on his lids.

His eyes closed, he released her hand and, blindly reaching out, put his arms around her. It seemed to him he held something wholly unknown in his arms, and making love to her would reveal it, reveal it in dimensions and depths he couldn't even now guess at, as he couldn't guess, really, what she would be like when he undressed her, for he couldn't be sure she didn't belong to a bright and inhuman sex to which he was drawn as he was drawn by gravity.

He wanted to see her naked. He wanted to hold her naked in his arms.

He asked, 'Will you come with me?'

She didn't answer, but didn't resist when he took her by the hand and guided her. He wouldn't look at her eyes.

He kissed the middle of her forehead, and a sensation as of

75

unlocked blood flowing to the surface of his body caused sudden expanding twinges at the back of his neck, in his armpits, in his groin, in his lungs, in his bowels. He ran a finger beneath the collar of her dress and touched the soft flesh which, lower down, would swell out into a round breast that was itself drawn out to the impossible softness of a nipple. He slowly undressed her. She lay limply. In her passivity, she seemed to be laying herself open to him to do whatever he wanted to her.

The passive openness reminded him all at once: but she was unwell. He pulled his hand away from her, and simply stared at her body, as though the awareness of her state were a warning that whatever he might do to her, he had no way of knowing how, finally, she would react.

The excited wonder − a wonder at her stillness belied by so many little movements in her breathing, her swallowing, her heatbeats, little jerks of her fingers and legs − made him lean over, lean close enough to sense his breath billowing back at him from her skin, and touch the angle of her thighbone with the tip of his tongue, expecting the slight wet contact to break up her stillness into a thrashing animation. But she remained still.

He ran his tongue down the angle of her thighbone into the hollow of her groin. As he did, he sensed her body go tight, and immediately sensed a contrary attempt to make it relax again, relax into a passivity he all at once realized was meant to be, not open in what it promised, but open as a blank sheet of paper was open, neither accepting him nor rejecting him. But she couldn't quite suppress the rigidity that stiffened her muscles as he, hedgingly, drew his tongue towards the centre of her groin, feeling tangled hairs drag at it.

He thought: he *would* make her react. She would not be able to suppress what he would do to her, even if he had to make sex bleed to do it.

Her body suddenly bucked, and bucked again, and she was not only thrusting her groin up into his face, she was pulling his head down to it by his hair. She yanked his head up, then pulled it towards her face, and he found himself sliding over her while she pulled his head from left to right and kissed him, kissed him on the ears, temples, eyes, nose, forehead, and forced her tongue between his teeth to press it against the roof of his mouth. Wet with sweat, he writhed on her body; her legs were raised, her arms bent back and raised to hold tightly to his hair, he was in a kind of crib, and she held him in it, sucking at his throat, sucking at his tongue.

She rolled him over and lay on him. All the while she kissed him she kept her eyes wide open and stared at him as if to keep always in focus the single-minded object of her involvement: this blank sex. She drew a little away from him to hang above him and make her elongated breasts swing across his chest; he not only felt his blood begin to drain away from his skin in reverse proportion to the way she was mentally insisting the blood should rise to her skin, he felt, lying on his back naked, stark in the glare of her eyes. She very slowly lowered herself on him, and the contact of the nipples on his chest made him try to press away and down into the bed. Her breasts bulged as she pressed nearer and nearer with an intent he could see in the muscles of her arms and shoulders. She was going to kiss him. He didn't want her to kiss him. He turned his head away. Just when he felt her breath on his cheek, however, he threw her over and, to keep her down, fell on her.

He thought: if she was going to be calculating in having sex, he would be more calculating. He would make love to her that she could not bear. He sucked at her throat, just under an ear, until an oval red-and-purple patch appeared. She struggled to get free, but he wouldn't let her. He sucked at her breast. By digging the heels of her feet into the tangled bedclothes, she tried to push herself out from under him, but he pulled her back. He lay on her, and grabbing at her throat with one hand so she started to gag, he was able, after many slipping attempts, to insert the head of his cock in her – he could, looking down,

see the glans being squeezed together by the lips of her vagina
– and thrust down into her. She moaned slightly, and he let go
of her throat.

'No,' she said.

He didn't answer. With each thrust of his hips, he felt her
body shudder. She rocked her head from side to side and flailed
her arms in jerks. Her hands clenched and unclenched, her feet
kicked, her ribs strained to rise out of her body like spikes. His
sweat dripped on her, and a pungent smell emanated about
them both. For a second they looked at one another, and in the
flash she saw in his eyes, as though they had gone blind, that
what he was doing was as beyond him as what she was doing
was beyond her; the horror of being in his arms passed
through her as she felt her body suddenly contract and violently expand, expand out and out, and she heard herself
shout, 'No! Oh no!'

He slept the night through beside her.

In the morning, she woke before he did. She got up quietly;
she didn't want to wake him. She bathed. All the thin films of
sex juices that made her skin tight dissolved into the water;
she lay for a long while. She thought she might leave the flat
before he woke; she didn't want to be there. Instead, she
stayed silently in the sitting-room. She heard him get up, go to
the bathroom, then go back to the bedroom. She didn't want
him to come into the room she was in; she didn't want to see
him. When he did come in, dressed, he hardly looked at her.
He sat. She shifted about on her seat. She was about to get up,
but remained. What she was most anxious about was that he
would begin to speak, that he might begin to tell her what he
thought and felt about what had happened; nothing had happened, she thought, about which he should have any thoughts
or feelings. From across the room he looked at her, looked at
her in such a way that she couldn't focus on him, and she had
to turn away.

She asked, 'Shall I prepare you something to eat?'

'No.' He said, 'I must leave. I must go to work.'

'I'll go to my flat,' she said.

'Stay here,' he said.

The sense of him and his silence remained in the flat after he left, and the chairs, rugs, the pictures, the books, the flute, the astrolabe, the oil lamp all became objects of the sense, all referred to him sitting, standing, looking about.

She walked around his flat, from room to room.

In the bedroom, she lay on the unmade bed. She felt suddenly exposed, as though she were naked and lying on a bed outside, and anyone could come up to her and do what he wanted to her. She wrapped a blanket around herself. She must do something, she thought, must at last decide either to protect herself from him or give in to him, though she had no idea what she would protect herself from or what she would be giving in to. She sensed, all about her, his vast, exposing silence, in which, as in darkness, he was, even away from her now, preparing for her what she didn't know. She wrapped herself up more tightly in the blanket. She waited for him to come back.

He was sitting next to her before the empty stage, expectant, excited. She didn't have to say a word. From the corner of his eye he saw her studying the old theatre, the little sharp lights behind crystal prisms, the people finding their seats. He pointed out a dark thin woman wearing a red-and-yellow embroidered cloak, the hood of which, circled by a fringe of dangling coins, was drawn about her face; whatever part of her face might have been exposed she kept covered by a long black hand.

Valerian saw Marion stare at the woman.

The musicians appeared. They sat, cross-legged, on rugs at the back of the stage and placed their instruments beside them. The lights dimmed. One of the musicians slowly rose. He stood motionless, waiting for the emergence on to the stage, in file, of the dancers, men wrapped in black cloaks, who promptly sat in a row at the side of the stage. There was a long pause, the dancers all bowed their heads, surmounted by tall round hats, to the ground, then the musician, still standing, began to chant. His voice was high, strident, and the warbles brought it to sudden higher pitches that were jolting; his long, long recitation seemed to revolve its dissonances, by its very length, into a rich, disembodied hum.

A single reed flute took over, took over as if abstracting some thin cry from the human voice and bringing it to where the voice couldn't go. The single reed was joined by more reeds, and, slowly – a tempo evolved not from any intention, but from the sheer chance conjunctions of added instruments producing sounds which, with constant repetition, became a tempo – shrill stringed instruments joined in, and drums tapped lightly, and small, hardly resonant brass cymbals.

The dancers suddenly rose when the tempo took over and seemed to detach itself from the musicians and to form a wide circle about which the dancers, with short, deliberate, springing steps, paced, one after the other, their long black cloaks, held closed about them, swaying, their tall dark brown hats bobbing; at an imperceptible signal, the dancers drew to the side of the stage and threw off their cloaks to reveal long white robes and pantaloons beneath gathered in at the ankles. Each dancer crossed his arms over his chest, clasping his shoulders. A master signalled one dancer, who advanced, his arms still crossed over his chest, bowed, was, it appeared, embraced by the master, and, at a tangent, moved off from the master, moved off as if he were a large, perfectly balanced sphere which, in glancing against the round bulk of the leader, began, began very slowly, to spin, then to spin, with the impetus of its own movement, faster, and the dancer's arms, with a delicate, gentle, unfolding gesture, gradually opened, opened wide, one hand pointing upward and the other pointing downward, and the skirt of the robe flared out into a spinning circle. Another dancer followed suit, and another, with a slowness in the unfolding, all the while the music repeating over and over the tempo until all the dancers, their arms outstretched, their skirts swelling, swirling, were spinning, were spinning with an ease, a quiet abandon to the music, which kept them concentric as they revolved in slow orbits about the stage, revolved around and around, and the dancers, by their very movement, ceased to be dancers, but vague globed shapes, and the music stopped, and the shapes continued, the only sound the sound of slippers brushing against the floor, continued to follow the tempo which the music had established but had brought to a point beyond which it could no longer follow, and all at once it seemed to Valerian that he, that Marion, that everyone in the theatre was moving too, moving round and round, and the motion itself was abstracted into an always deeper stillness, a space into which they, their seats, the theatre were irresistibly drawn, in which they became points in a vast geometric zodiac, a space that curved away and far beyond them.

Something came over Valerian that, in the urgency with which his muscles responded to it, made him want to touch someone. He turned to Marion, whose eyes, large, were staring through tears.

They walked along the paved embankment of the river, where strings of sharp white lights were looped from lamp to lamp; the lights shook in the wind, and made Marion's and Valerian's shadows waver.

They climbed stairs to the bridge. Other people were hurrying, as if to keep ahead of the cold wind. Marion held Valerian's arm, and they walked slowly. They were, Valerian thought, in a dark and heavy-bottomed sphere which isolated them and made them move slowly. Perhaps the sphere was nothing but their silence since the end of the performance, when they got up from their seats, put on their coats, and left the hall. At least the sphere was porous enough to allow the wind through; it made their clothes flap.

When Valerian finally spoke, it seemed to him his voice boomed in the wind and echoed down the wide swift river. 'Now will you tell me if you'll come away or not?'

She shook her head. 'There's nothing I can say.'

'Perhaps you won't ever make up your mind.'

She didn't answer. On the inside of their enclosing sphere he imagined he could see the slow and unintelligible patterns of Marion's thoughts, but he knew that if he asked her what she was thinking she would say, 'Nothing.'

He wondered if he was becoming like Jonathan, who had finally to take her negative answers for granted. He thought: no, because the essential difference between him and Jonathan was that Jonathan could not bear her not telling him exactly what was on her mind, while Valerian knew that for himself he did not want her to tell him, even if he asked.

She said, 'Once, when I took a walk with Jonathan, we crossed this bridge.'

'I was thinking about him,' Valerian said. 'Isn't that strange?'

'It isn't strange at all,' she said.

They walked on.

'He was, in a way, extraordinary,' Valerian said.

'In what way?'

Valerian thought, but didn't say: in being drawn to you. He said, 'In going as far as he did.'

Valerian sensed the heavy patterns shift slightly. 'Do you mean with me?' she asked.

'Perhaps,' he said.

'He at least knew enough to break off before going too far.'

'What does that mean?' he asked.

'He left when he realized it was clearly possible for him to become like me.'

'To become unwell?'

She gave him a look that was like a sharp slash across her eyes. 'Who said that? Who said I'm unwell? It was he who was unwell, sick with believing I could, that I even wanted to, change.'

'You don't think you're unwell?'

'I don't think I'm anything.'

The wind blew about them, making the suspension bridge

sway and buffeting the palely illuminated river below in rough patches.

Valerian asked, 'What about me? Do you think I'm unwell?'

She said nothing.

The wind hit him hard in the face. 'The fact is I am,' he said.

'If that's what you think –' she said.

'It has nothing to do with what I decide. I am.'

'Maybe,' she said, 'just sick with wanting to be sick.'

About to speak, the wind rushed into his open mouth and down his throat. 'No. I don't want to be.'

'You want to be,' she said.

'You won't believe there are things that one can't help, that go beyond one's wanting them or not?'

She didn't answer.

He stopped her by putting his hand on her arm. They stood just where a flight of cement stairs led down from the bridge to the sidewalk below. 'There are things,' he said, 'and they're undeniable.'

She looked from him to the cement walls on either side of the flight of steps on which large graffiti were drawn with chalk and the fuzzy lines sprayed from aerosol tins of paint; in the midst of the tangled slogans and drawings was a huge red erect cock stuck into an oval cunt. She pointed it out. 'As undeniable as that?'

'More than that,' he said.

'As what? As death?'

He said, suddenly, 'I love you.' He reached out to grab her shoulders and pull her to him. 'I love you – that's my hideous sickness.'

She turned away and, reaching out her hand, touched a cement wall. On contact, she felt rebound from the wall towards Valerian a surge of such twisted feelings that the only one she could make out was a feeling as hard and flat and impenetrable as the wall itself, against which he could bash himself to death. She despised him, she would destroy him. She didn't move, but pressed her fingertips harder against the cement, thinking: she must control this hatred, must, when she turned to him, turn to him a look of zero —

Facing him, she imagined a great round zero surrounded her, the circumference touching her head and feet, and he would not be able to see beyond it, would not be able to see her, would only be able to see the empty zero, as empty and as black as the black zeros of her eyes.

But immediately she saw that he had not understood. He saw the zeros — they were visibly reflected in his eyes — but she recognized that he saw them not as an end; her great round zero meant to him that everything was open.

To move her, he took her by the arm and led her down to the street.

Before her door, she fumbled for her key; when she found it, she couldn't get it into the lock. He gently extracted it from her hand, unlocked, and showed her into her own flat.

He brought her into the sitting-room. She watched his actions, his gestures, as from a great distance. She sat.

He stood over her. He said, 'You'll come with me.'

His voice, too, seemed to come from a great distance; she was not sure she had heard.

'Come where?' she asked dumbly.

'With me.'

She wondered if he meant now. Now, she couldn't move. She rolled her head against the back of the armchair.

He said, 'You see now you have no reason at all for not coming. You must see it.'

She simply rolled her head from side to side.

'Say you'll come.'

She said, 'I don't care what you do to me.' She closed her eyes.

She heard him say, 'Then you'll come.'

She felt her body seem to collapse into the chair. When she sensed him come closer, kneel by her, lean close, so his breath was exhaled on the side of her face, she thought: she must get up. But she couldn't make herself move. She imagined his features, near her, enormous: his huge eyes, his nose, his mouth. It was as if, her own eyes closed, she were still able to see him, but she wasn't able to do anything to stop him from pressing nearer. She was open to him; he would take her wherever he wanted, and do to her whatever he wanted – he would because he could see there was nothing to stop him. She opened her eyes and looked at him in a way that made him ask:

'What's wrong?'

'You don't know what you're getting yourself into,' she said.

'No,' he said, 'I don't.'

'You should go away.'

'We'll both go away.'

'You've made up your mind, have you?'

'Yes,' he said. 'I'll take you.'

She shook her head.

'I will,' he said, 'and you'll come.'

'I don't care where I am.'

'You'll be with me,' he said.

She was not sure if the low faint groan she heard came from her throat.

He said, 'Now, you'll go to bed.'

She waited for him to leave her, but he only stood back and looked down at her, as if examining her, and she realized that he wouldn't go until he saw that she was in bed.

She pulled herself up from the chair and went into the bedroom. Valerian followed. He watched her slowly undress. He watched her get into bed. She lay flat, the blankets up to her chin.

Her hair was tangled on the pillow; he wanted to tug at it. She wasn't looking at him, but at the wall on the opposite side of the room.

She knew that he was waiting for something to happen before he left. It wouldn't come from her; she couldn't make anything happen. Then, quickly, she glanced at him, and she saw in his face, his hands, that he was about to make it happen. She drew back from what he would do when he leaned over her; his lips grazed her hands, which she had instinctively placed over her face to guard herself against him.

Her hands went rigid when he placed his on hers and lifted them from her face. She lay still. He lowered his head and kissed her on the mouth. He drew away.

She said, 'You'll never get from me what you want.'

'Yes,' he said.

'You'll wait?'

'Not so long,' he answered. 'I'll get it.'

She shook her head.

'You'll give it to me,' he said.

She shook her head again.

He said, 'You won't be able to keep it from me.'

Walking to his flat, down the empty street, he felt as alone as when he was with Marion; he was always alone with her, and he had no idea what, alone, he would do with her. Yes, he thought, everything was open, and it was all dark. He had only this: the sense that he loved her, that he wanted her, senses which, in themselves, he could not understand any more than he could understand why he should want her, dead to him, to love him. He'd wait for it; he would wait until she could no longer bear not to give it.

His sheets, as he got into bed, felt damp and cold.

The train was late in leaving. There were many people in the corridor jogging past him as he stood before the window and looked out. Finally, he sensed a tugging pull, and dark pillars and posts strung with looping wires passed slowly, then more swiftly, then were violently caught back by the increasing velocity of the train. The city was shaken from the steel sides: an illuminated viaduct, the pale neon-red of a hotel front, a street-light showing an unfinished apartment house.

The train burst into the quiet of the countryside.

The night was enormous. All he could see were flat fields and occasionally the headlights of a car searching a row of houses, a wall, a distant line of trees. By refocusing his eyes he saw in reflection the compartment behind him, where Marion was sitting on the edge of his made-up berth. In the reflection, she stood, looked around, and came towards him.

They both stared out. Valerian's thinking was absorbed by the long distance before them, the space they were travelling through. The other passengers left the corridor and went into their compartments. A conductor passed through, shutting behind him the metal doors at the ends of the wagon.

Valerian finally said, 'Perhaps we should go to sleep.'

She went before him. He slid closed the compartment door and pulled the shades. They stood very close to one another in the narrow space.

She washed at the little basin in the corner of the compartment. He saw her backbone and the angles of her shoulder blades moving as she moved. It seemed to him he watched her through deep layers of glass which would prevent him from touching her even if he wanted to. But he didn't want to. He watched her dry her face and, not looking at him, slip into her berth. He washed. The water sloshed in the basin. He was conscious of her looking at his bare back, buttocks, legs. The towel in his hands, he turned to her. She was looking up. He sat on the edge of her berth, but she still did not look at him. The tip of his penis touched the cold metal.

He didn't know if she was waiting for him to say something, to do something. He tried to think of something to say, of a gesture he might make, but there was nothing he wanted to talk to her about, and he did not want her to think that any of his gestures might mean that he wanted to make love. He rose from the edge of the berth and climbed the little ladder to his own.

He could feel the tremendous rhythmic movement of the train as he lay. It was a rhythm he could easily give in to, at once powerful, constant, a rattling, buoying sway, a motion as deep as the sleep opening up beneath him. Awake, he would strain a little against a sudden acceleration, or lean to the opposite direction of a curve, as if his tiny movement could exert a control over the long string of wagons; but now he gave into the thundering of the train, and he felt, as his mind sped into darkness, a rush that made the wheels skim the tracks, almost on the point of derailing the train and making it fly out sail-like.

He woke when the train stopped – not at a station, for there were no shattering noises outside of people getting on or off. Instead, he heard through the open window an immense country silence swollen with the *cri cri* of crickets, the owls, the long, ascending cries of night birds. The train stood anchored in the middle of the country, waiting, he thought, for a train coming in the opposite direction to pass before it could speed through. He could smell coolness blowing in through the thin shade covering the window. He imagined the entire still train filled with bodies, sleeping.

He was falling asleep again. He thought he heard voices, and he snatched his mind back from sleep to listen. It wasn't voices, it was vague outside sounds. Then he heard a train whistle shriek through the night. It was answered by another distant whistle from an oncoming train which passed with a sudden bursting roar. The silence following sank like a weight, but it lasted only a moment before the train began again with a jolt.

He lay quietly, his eyes staring dimly upward. When he closed his eyes and pulled the blanket further up on his shoulder, he fell suddenly asleep, and the last he heard was the whistle echoing in a tunnel as the train passed through a mountain and out into the silence of a valley.

Again he woke to find the train had stopped. He was warm. The air seemed as inert as the train itself. He drew his arms out from beneath the blanket and folded his hands under his head. This time he heard voices outside, and the sound of the metal bars being struck against the wheels. Occasionally a lantern was flashed across the shade. The train was shunted back and forth, the voices rose at times to shouts, and twice someone passed down the corridor outside the compartment. Then there was silence and stillness, both magnifying the tiny sounds of insects and water dripping. It occurred to him suddenly that he could not hear Marion breathing. He sat up quickly. He looked over the edge of the berth and down at her. In the dim blue light, he saw her, but it was a long time before he could make out that her chest was heaving slightly, because he still couldn't hear her.

Through eyes narrowed to slits, she saw his dark head leaning over the edge of the upper berth; she couldn't make out his features. She held her breath. She had not been able to sleep because of the movement of the train. She wondered, now, where she was. Valerian's head hung above her; it might have been the head of a stranger peering down at her. She couldn't hold her breath any longer. She tried to breathe as she would in sleep, and Valerian's head drew away.

She thought, as she had thought again and again over the night : she had put herself into the hands of a stranger, and she was, and would be even more so, isolated with him without being able to get away. And why, she wondered, now that she knew it was too late, should she ask herself, again and again, why she had come? She heard him moving above her.

He could not bear the immobility of the train. He threw off the sheet and crawled to the end of the berth. He reached down to lift the shade. He leaned out. In the pre dawn, he could just make out a stream and clumps of long reeds, an iron grid bridge with a level crossing over it, and a road curving up from it to a dark mountain.

Marion stood with the luggage by a high spiked iron fence. Behind it, steam hissed about the trains. The great echoing space of the station was complicated by hanging wires, girders, signs. Valerian had left her. She tried to see over the heads of the massed people to find him.

She caught, in the crowd, the eye of a man staring at her. She turned away quickly, and just as quickly glanced back to find he was still staring at her. She looked at the luggage.

When she glanced up, in another direction, she caught another man staring at her, and then others, men and women.

She tried to keep herself from seeing them, but all the eyes on her, from a multitude of angles, made her aware of her shoes, buttons, fingernails, neck, ears, hairs, all the exposed bits of herself which, if she let them, would confuse her for the attention they drew to themselves. A moment later, her arms raised and pressed across her breasts, she forced herself into the crowd.

She had no idea where to go to find Valerian, and squeezed through the people, all moving slowly in different directions.

She freed herself from the crowd by passing through a doorway from which a grille had been pulled back. She stepped into a large room piled high with crates. A man immediately came from behind a pile and motioned to her that she wasn't allowed there. She walked past him to an open door that led out to the street.

The narrow street led to a square in front of the station. There was a crowd of men at a corner of the square, beneath a ragged tree. She went quickly into the station again, the front part less crowded, but she didn't see Valerian.

She hurried down a corridor lined with lockers on either side, at the end of which was a left-luggage office. She turned back, and the corridor took her to a bare room covered, floor, walls, ceiling, in white tiles and smelling of urine. She came out.

She managed to get herself to a part of the station where there were stands of magazines and newspapers everywhere. She walked among the stands, and, noticing that people were staring at her even now, she realized she was making awkward, rapid movements. She stopped. She pulled her hair back. She turned, and there, facing her from across the shiny marble floor, was Valerian. He didn't move; he simply looked at her, and she imagined she saw him smiling.

All her muscles tightened up more. She didn't know if she should go to him or walk away; she didn't know what he, motionless, was waiting for her to do.

As she stood, watching him, she felt her muscles suddenly unclench, and for a moment she was weak; then, just as suddenly, her muscles drew her up as if they had tensed in a way that drew together emotions she hardly recognized.

She saw, all at once, in his very stance, in his smile, in the way he looked at her and waited for her to come to him, that he had done what he had wanted to do : he had succeeded in involving her in something she couldn't get out of.

She approached him, her incoherent emotions pressed back by a stark calm.

She couldn't, now, get out, she thought, but she would finally.

In the hotel, in the middle of the city, she asked, 'Will we be here long?'

'Until the boat leaves. Would you prefer not to be here?'

'No,' she said. She went out on to the narrow balcony of their hotel room. The shadows of the buildings were cast half way across the wide promenade down the centre of the avenue. In the slanting shade, the people and the traffic below appeared sharp and clear, but in the sunlight on the other side of the avenue the air was almost opaque with bright floating dust particles and fumes in which the pedestrians and cars disappeared. The heat, the smell of exhaust, the noise of traffic, children shouting, seemed to her to rise up from the sunlit side, while the shadows remained quiet and still. She saw an old woman in black, carrying a cage with a canary in it, pass from the shadows into the blinding sunlight, and just as she dissolved a young man emerged from the sunlight and came into the shadows carrying a caged canary. He came to the edge of the promenade where there was a little bird market. Marion turned to Valerian, who was standing behind him.

'You think you're showing me something I don't know by bringing me here,' she said. 'In fact, I was here before.'

His only reaction was to draw near her. 'A long time ago?'

'Yes.'

'And do you recall it?'

'I can hardly recall it but for vague impressions.'

'What impressions?' he asked.

She shrugged her shoulders and said she would like to wash. He stepped aside to let her come in from the balcony.

'What impressions?' he asked again.

She sat on the bed. She closed her eyes for a second, then said, 'Nothing.'

'Nothing?'

'No: an old tower with a gateway through it.'

'Where is it, do you think?' he asked.

'Near a market perhaps, where there were stalls with canvas awnings. There was straw on the cobbles, and crates of oranges.'

'I don't remember that.'

'No? Perhaps it was a covered market, with a grimy glass dome, and all the stalls were under grid arches.'

'Cast iron arches, with iron flowers and vines decorating the posts?'

'No, I don't think so,' she said. 'But I recall slabs of marble with water running down them to keep the fish fresh.'

'In the fish market,' he said.

'Yes,' she said doubtfully.

'By the sea.'

'Yes, by the sea. Yes, I recall the sea-front. I recall the oil slick on the water and the narrow streets, and at night the bars.'

'The bars?'

'Yes.' She paused for only a second. 'I recall going down a dark street and passing a huge apartment house, and through

92

the open door, past dirty, paint-peeling staircases and a broken-down bicycle and baskets and clothes lines, I saw a little scruffy illuminated garden with a couple of rickety tables where men were sitting and drinking and a very fat woman was dancing.'

'That must have been another city.'

'I think it was this one.'

'Perhaps,' he said.

'The women are very fat,' she said.

He smiled. 'And the men are thin.'

'Gaunt. The men look very hard at you as you pass their bars. I went into a bar once.'

'What did they do?'

'They looked hard at me.'

'Did you stay?'

'I had a glass of wine or an aperitif or maybe a very sweet and heavy liqueur half of which stuck to the inside of the small glass. There was an acrid smell in the bar, as of wine gone sour.'

She got up.

'And what else?' Valerian asked.

'I remember a gaunt man with a scar right across his forehead. He was in the bar.'

'Were you young then?'

'Yes. I wanted to see everything. He said something to me, but I didn't understand, or didn't allow myself to understand.'

'Do you regret it now?'

'No, not now. I did then. I regretted turning away from him as I was in the act of turning away. Now, I think: what could he have done to me that made me turn away from him? Nothing I can imagine, and that's why, now, I don't regret turning away, because, ultimately, he was just a man.'

'Perhaps not.'

She shook her head. 'He gave me a card. It was an invitation to visit a leather factory.'

'Did you go?'

'Yes. It was right in the middle of the city, in a horrible, run-down warehouse. I saw him, but I didn't make any sign of recognition, and he didn't see me.'

'That was the only personal contact you had?'

'Hardly personal, but yes.' She paused. 'I wandered the city.'

'None of which you've just made up?'

'You think I've made it up because I can't recall the details accurately.'

'You've been accurate enough,' he said. 'What other impressions do you retain?'

'Why don't you tell me yours.'

'I want to know yours.'

She walked about the room.

'I recall fountains – no, not fountains, but, on street corners, spigots sticking out of the open mouth of a worn stone face, or the bung-hole of a stone casket, or the lip of a stone pitcher, from which water gushed into a trough and overflowed into the gutter. The water was tepid to drink.'

'And old women filling big green bottles?'

'I suppose. But that's enough.'

'No. Tell me more.'

'But you can *see* the city.' She pointed. 'It's just outside.'

'I want to hear about your city.'

'It isn't my city.'

'It's your city.'

'Is any city I vaguely recall my city?'

'Isn't it?'

She went to the balcony again.

'What else do you recall?' he asked.

She didn't answer for a while. The slanting shadows cut further across the avenue. 'The light,' she said, 'the light that seemed not to show up things, but dissolve them, like a gas.'

He came up behind her. 'And the heat?'

'Yes.' She put her hand to her throat. 'I recall the heat, above all.'

There was a long pause. She could feel his breath on her

94

neck. The he said, 'In fact, you've never been in this city, have you?'

She turned around to look at him. 'Why do you say that?'

'Because I know you've made it all up.'

She looked away. 'Yes,' she said.

'Why did you say you'd been?' he asked.

She didn't answer.

'It doesn't matter,' he said. 'But there is still the city I know.'

The city he knows? she thought, again standing on the balcony, waiting for him to wash and change. The city he knows? Even if the whole place were dismantled and he could from memory identify each stone, each paving block, each window cornice, rebuilding the city entire again, he could not say that the city he knew was any more the real city than the city she had tried to impress him with knowing, because both his city and hers were as illusory as their forced thinking. When he came out of the bathroom, she said:

'I'm too tired to go out.'

'We could go to a quiet place,' he said.

'Where?'

'To a bar.'

In the bar, Valerian took from the inside pocket of his jacket a street map of the city which he spread open on the little round table between them. Their drinks stood on either side of the map. Marion was annoyed not only at his marking off the places he would take her to see, she was annoyed at what she could only think of as the presumption of the map itself to be a miniature abstract of the city, the presumption that the lines referred to streets and squares and buildings outside. She should have insisted that she *had* been to the city before, that she knew it as well as he, and that he and the map were wrong to suppose a little dark rectangle should mark the actual site of a park. She had relinquished the city to him and his map. It was his, it was the map's. She resented him and it to the point of deliberate inattentiveness. She looked about.

She noted, standing at the bar, a tall, rather gaunt man who turned to her just as she saw him. Across his forehead, from temple to temple, was a straight, thin scar. She quickly dropped her eyes.

Each time she glanced up at him he was staring at her, as if she had, by catching his eye first, given him the right to, and each time their eyes met she gave him more and more right. She felt her hands and feet go cold, and when he turned fully towards her, leaning on the bar with his elbow, the cold rose into her arms and legs.

She tried to stare at Valerian's map. He had put little black x's here and there on it. It occurred to her that she did not want Valerian to see the man. She glanced up at him again. The man was looking down to the floor, so all she could see of his face was his forehead, smooth beneath his dark hair, cut across by the line of the scar, so straight she wondered if it might be a kind of ceremonial scar. Suddenly, he was looking at her and smiling. Her lips twitched. She looked at Valerian, still busy on the map, and, with a reversal of all her feelings, she thought: no, Valerian must see him. She turned to the man and smiled, but smiled as into a large, crowded room where she could not see anyone in particular.

He came out of the crowd. She only saw him when he was standing above her, leaning slightly, and saying, 'I think, perhaps, we have met.' All she really saw was the scar. She turned immediately to Valerian, who, pencil pointing to an x on the map, was staring at the man, staring, Marion saw, at his forehead, with a suspension of any reaction. Marion looked back at the man. She said, or heard herself say, 'Perhaps.'

The man asked, shifting only his eyes towards Valerian, 'I do not recall that you were married when I last saw you. Is this your husband?'

Marion too shifted only her eyes towards Valerian and could see but the blur of his face in the periphery of her vision. 'No,' she said, 'I'm not married.'

The man bowed a little, or perhaps inclined his head to come nearer her. 'A friend, then?'

'Yes,' Marion said.

'May I ask you and your friend to join me in a drink?'

Now Marion turned fully to face Valerian, who did not seem to be seeing her, but some presence directly behind her.

She asked him, 'Would you want to?'

He refocused his eyes to see her. 'If you would like.'

She asked the man to sit. He did, and signalled for a waiter to come and take orders. He glanced at Valerian's map and said, 'You don't know the city?'

'I know it.'

'If you know it, why do you need a plan?'

Valerian folded his map and slipped it in the pocket inside his jacket.

The man turned to Marion.

She said, 'I don't know it. I've never before been in this city.'

He paused for a second, a little lost. 'Then we must have met in another.'

'Yes.'

The waiter came with the drinks, placed them on the table, took the empty glasses and, before withdrawing, spoke close to the ear of the man with the scar, who rose. 'You'll excuse me for a moment,' he said, and left.

Marion saw him pick up a telephone receiver from the bar and hold it to his ear. At that moment, she heard Valerian say:

'You must know that you're free.'

She kept looking at the man. 'Does that need saying?'

His silence was a concession that, no, it didn't need saying. Neither said anything more, and Marion could sense the silence deepen with Valerian's palpable expectation of what would happen when the man came back. He came back presenting an expression as thin and sharp as his scar. He said:

'I have a few hours and a car. What I know of the city may not be very special, but it is not easily accessible. Will you allow me to show you?'

Valerian said nothing.

Marion looked at him for a moment, then back to the man. 'I think my friend wouldn't be interested,' she said.

'He prefers to do it on his own?'

The man, Marion thought, imagined he held in his hands a long cord which, with great tugs, he was pulling in with the confidence that she was attached to the end of it.

She said, 'No. He would prefer not to do it with you.'

The man smiled a little crookedly. 'And you?'

Again, Marion looked at Valerian, who appeared not to be hearing what was being said until she asked him, 'Would you mind?' and he looked at her as with a sudden and open surprise that she should have asked, his eyes looking everywhere but at her, his voice sharp with his disassociation. 'Why should I mind?'

Rising, she said, 'Then I'll see you at the hotel.'

She found him lying on one of the two narrow beds in the hotel room. He stood – almost jumped up – when she came in.

She went around to her bed and lay on it. She closed her eyes. When she opened them she saw Valerian still standing where he had been and looking down at her.

He cleared his throat, making his voice even. 'What did you see?'

'Practically everything, I should think.'

'In three hours?'

'We went by car.'

'Nothing struck you?'

'No.'

He sat at the edge of his bed. 'Did you stop?'

She simply continued to look at him.

'Where did you stop?' he asked.

'At his flat,' she said.

'Oh.' He got up. She saw him from the corner of her eye. He seemed to be wondering why he had got up and which way he should turn; he turned in two or three directions, then remained still. He asked, 'What was his name?'

'I don't know.'

'You won't see him again?'

'No.' There was a long pause. 'What did you do?' she asked.

'Nothing,' he said.

'You stayed in the room?'

'I slept.'

'I'd like to sleep,' she said.

'Then you should.'

She felt very heavy, too heavy to move and the heaviness seemed to her sticky and damp. 'I would like to have a shower,' she said.

'And then you can sleep.'

'For a little.' She got up laboriously. As she was passing him, she said, 'You know, I had never met him before.'

'It doesn't matter,' he said.

She stood by him a moment. 'No, of course it doesn't,' she said, and while she was showering, she thought: no, he doesn't, it doesn't.

They had dinner in the hotel. They were silent throughout, as if someone were sitting with them, Marion thought, but not the man with the scar, because the presence was that of someone close to them who was about to die, and they were both aware there was nothing they could say that would be equal to that.

Back in their room, Valerian prepared to go to sleep while Marion sat in an armchair. They had not put the lights on. It was enough that street-lights and the light from neon signs were blasted in through the slats of the shutters by the noise of cars and motorbikes and loud voices from below. The light and the noise were all the evidence they had that there was in fact a city outside. Marion didn't want to think about it. She clasped her neck in her hands and rocked back and forth. She continued to sit, rocking, after he got into bed.

He watched her. She appeared to be bound tightly by the

stripes of light, from which she was trying to free herself. He let her be. He wouldn't touch her.

She knew he would avoid taking her into the main parts of the city. He took her, in the morning, to a market which occupied a bare, littered area beneath an old wall.

Valerian stopped at a table, made of planks placed across wooden horses, on which there were piles of old books and magazines. Marion left him. An old woman sitting on her haunches at the corner of a blanket motioned her over. The woman pointed to a collection of silver chains lined up on the blanket. She picked up one and dangled it in front of Marion. Marion shook her head. For a second, it came over her that Valerian had left her, and she turned back to find him. He was still brooding over the books. She saw him look up from them and search the sparse crowd before he saw her. She went to him.

'Look!' he said.

He had a large parchment-covered book before him. The parchment was battered and scratched. He opened the book at the back and slowly turned the pages. They appeared as if they had been soaked and, in drying, warped. A smell of dust rose up. She did not recognize the script, which was in long columns. He turned to a full-page picture of two intersecting circles; the eye-shaped space of the intersection was vivid blue, and the top circle, above the intersection, was red, the lower circle yellow; the background was a pale blue. He kept the page open, but said nothing. He turned it.

He paused at the next picture. A woman, her naked angular body bright red, the tips of her toes and fingers blue, was drawn with one leg raised, her arms akimbo. Her hair was flying out. She was meant to be dancing.

The next picture Valerian paused at, towards the end of the book, really at the front of the book, showed a group of pale green men sitting in a circle: one man held up a bell, another was blowing a flute, another was plucking with long curved fingers some flat stringed instrument at his feet, another's hand was posed on the top of a small drum.

Valerian closed the book, turned to her and smiled, and she saw in his smile what she had never before seen with such clarity: a sudden promise that he had discovered something that would make a difference to them both.

Aboard the ship, they walked the deck in a slow, criss-crossing dance step to the ship's lurching.

'Why don't you tell me?' she asked.

'Because I don't want you to make up your mind about it,' Valerian said.

'It?' she said. 'It? Can't you be a little more precise than that?'

He saw her smile.

'If I told you,' he said, 'you'd only kill it.'

Her smile increased. 'By making up my mind about it?'

'By not giving it a chance.'

'And so you'll keep it back from me? You'll keep me guessing?'

He said nothing. She suddenly stopped at the rail. He watched her look out at the dark sea. They could have been anywhere, he thought. She said:

'And what it is you're keeping from me – do you really know what it is?'

'I have a sense,' he said.

'That's not very strong, a sense,' she said. 'I'd like to think it was a bit more definite than that. There's nothing you can point to that would refer to it, nothing you can mark with a little x, knowing what the x stands for?'

'No.'

'Then you really don't know what you're talking about.'

Valerian remained silent, and so did Marion until, her smile forcing its way up into her cheeks, she said:

'It's dark.'

'Yes,' he said.

He saw that she was pursing her lips to keep herself from smiling. 'You agree?'

He thought: she was leading him on, but all he could make

out of her intention was a tensing derisiveness. He, in any case, felt tense.

'Yes,' he said, 'it's dark.'

She said, 'What do you imagine *is* dark? *It?*' She was not looking at him, but he saw her eyes glisten.

He said calmly, 'The night.'

'But if it happens to be very cloudy during the day, you can still say, "It's dark." '

'Yes,' he said.

'Do you imagine it's the air that's dark?'

'I don't know.'

'I'd like to know, but I don't suppose I ever will.' She turned to him. 'You must know.'

He frowned. 'I don't know,' he said.

She was about to laugh, but his look stopped her. She had been joking, had perhaps been trying to make a fool of him, but he already knew, she saw, that he was a fool. He was a fool for being with her at that very moment. He knew it, and she knew it. She made him a fool.

She put her hands on the rail.

She thought: it came to her often that she didn't know anything about Valerian; it came to her now that he didn't know anything about her. He thought that he would get to the end of her, but he didn't know the depths of her resources; he thought that he would uncover something that would engage her, but he didn't know the power of her disinterest. A sense of her darkness rose up to her as if from the sea and the night and she felt very heavy. She felt that her presence was very heavy, that it made the air heavy. He had asked her once to come away with him for his sake; she should have done everything possible to stay away for his sake. She wanted to tell him that she was aware of what he had taken on, but she didn't have to tell him; she knew they were both thinking of the same thing.

She said, suddenly, 'Whatever it is you're keeping from me, please don't think it will change me.'

'Perhaps you don't want to change,' he said.

'To want to I'd have to think it were possible.'

'It is.'

'Is it?'

'If I could show you that it is –'

'It's only killing me that will show me, and then I'll be beyond knowing in any case,' she said.

'Do you want to die?' he asked.

His answer was met by silence. He could feel her at once withdraw, all her still faintly echoing voice and derision rushing as into a vacuum.

'Do you?' he repeated.

Again, she said nothing.

He said, 'I know: you do.'

It was as if an immense ease came over him.

'You do,' he said again.

He put his hand on her wrist, then grasped it and pulled her towards him. Only her arm moved, extended limply from her shoulder to his hand clutching her wrist. For a moment her body was rigid, then she pulled against her own arm as though to leave it torn away and hanging from his hand so she could get away from him. The more she pulled the more he tightened his grasp. She said, 'Please, please don't,' and he let go. Her arm fell to her side.

She left him. She felt hollow and weak inside. She went quickly to the cabin and lay down.

It was as though he had got something from her she had been hiding, she thought; she had not been hiding, she never hid, anything. Why then did she feel so empty?

He made her feel empty. It was as though something had suddenly become clear in what he saw in her, and he took it. He imagined he now knew everything about her, and he would use it to get what he wanted from her. He would, with it, force her to some inevitable end staring backwards like an eye, would bring her to a point from which she would not be able to turn away. She imagined him pushing her down a tunnel, and she, finally, allowing him to because she realized that down the tunnel was the only possible direction she could go.

She looked up at the black round portholes. She was very hot and sweating. She knelt on her bed and tried to open a porthole, but the screws were so thickly covered with paint she couldn't move them. She lay back. She tried to control her muscles. All she could think to do was to appear asleep when Valerian came into the cabin.

Valerian remained where she had left him by the rail. There was all about him, he thought, a palpable atmosphere in which he would float off if he did not hold to the rail, an atmosphere made up, not of the sea air, the water, the darkness, but of something unnamable, and he would never be able to convince her of it. Oh, *it*! How did he allow her to prod him into going even so far? He leaned a little over the rail. He saw the lights from portholes projected on to the sea, making him imagine for a second that the ship was still, and the sea, visible through a series of luminous holes, was streaking past. One of the holes went dark. He closed his eyes. He listened.

He heard a slight hum. It grew in intensity with his awareness of it. He opened his eyes. The hum continued. He could not identify it. He tried to distinguish among all the other mixing sounds to isolate the hum. He noted the breeze flapping the canvas awnings put up for deck travellers, the smack of waves, the slurring of the ship's wake, the gurgling of water running overboard out of the drains, the whoosh and thump of the bow, distant, small voices, a general creaking and clanking, wind booming across the top of the smokestack, the engines. He listened carefully until it seemed to him that the hum was a tinnitus swelling out from an unknown source and that it itself was what evolved the other sounds and rhythms he heard, was what caused the *slush slush* of the wake, the pounding of the motor, the hollow boom of the wind, like an unlocatable pulse extending itself through the air, a pulse which could increase, or reverse itself, or cease altogether, and everything precariously dependent on it would also throb more intensely, or change its tempo, or stop.

He thought: he was a product of what he felt about Marion, as the flapping, the gurgling, the slurring, the whoosh and thump were products of the tinnitus; he and the night and the sea and the sky around him were but configured waves emanating from the obsessive sense he had of her: his love.

Valerian opened the doors and windows of the small house. He took the luggage into the bedroom. He saw Marion, behind him, look at the uncovered mattress of the bed.

She said, 'I think it'd be better if I slept alone.'

'We'll both sleep here,' he answered.

She twisted and turned. He lay at the edge, awake most of the night. When her foot or hand brushed against him, he didn't move.

He woke before she did. When she opened her eyes, she saw his eyes, distant. She could smell him. She ran her tongue over her dry lips. The sheet, when she moved, slid against her skin as though the cloth, too, were a sensitive skin. She stretched. Valerian remained still.

She got up, not speaking, and left the bedroom.

After a while, Valerian rose and went to the bathroom door. From inside, she sensed his presence outside. He suddenly opened the door. She was standing before the basin, looking in the mirror. She immediately turned away. He stood before her.

'Get out,' she said.

'You were in here a long time,' he said.

'Get out,' she said again.

He shook his head.

'You've got to leave me alone.'

'No.'

They remained motionless. She noted, in the stillness, his eyes, his lips, his neck. He took a small step towards her, and she went rigid. He stopped. She waited for him to come closer, but he didn't. He stepped back, and she felt her body step forward.

'You think I'll do something to myself.'

'I have no idea,' he answered.

'It's what you're waiting for.'

He smiled. 'No. Not that.'

She leaned closer to him, and for a second she thought she might be falling towards him, into his enveloping body odour. He drew away. She realized she had been about to press a finger to the hollow at the base of his throat. She grasped her right wrist in her left hand.

'I want to go back to bed until it gets too hot,' she said.

'You can do what you want.'

She knew he would follow her.

It was already too hot for the sheet. She couldn't sleep. She kept shifting position, while Valerian lay without moving. She could hardly bear the still presence of his body beside her.

He knew, as he lay, that she was watching him, anticipating the smallest movement of a hand or leg towards her. The only movement he made was to turn over on to his stomach.

Marion rode ahead of him on her bicycle.

The sunlight was so intense, it made the flat landscape colourless, the empty sky black. In the middle of a dry field they passed a tree, its branches twisted in one direction as if wind were blowing through it, but there was no wind.

Around a bend, the sea came into view, visible from the height as a vaporous whiteness. The fields they bicycled over became broad, slanting; horses stood motionless or the sheep bounded away. As they approached the sea the sky appeared vaster, blacker.

They parked their bikes beside a dusty bush. The wide, sea-corroded headland they crossed appeared to be made of the fossils of broken and splintered bones – vertebrae, pelvises, skulls, femurs – which lay embedded together in a great mass over which Valerian and Marion walked, avoiding the sharp edges and hollows. In places, the rock looked as porous as dry marrow. A smell of iodine rose up.

All about them, in shallow cavities, were rock pools encrusted with salt crystals. The salt was like snow, and for a sharp, displacing moment Valerian imagined that the intensity of the heat could have been the intensity of cold. Marion stayed close to him.

He spread a towel on a patch of sand and lay flat. Sweat streaked across his body. He squinted against the shattering sunlight and saw Marion lie beside him. Her body, stretched out, seemed to him very naked. He turned over on to his stomach. Now and then the sunlight hit him in blows, like a cold wind, and a shiver passed through him. He half fell asleep, fell into a feverish state, and he imagined his body and mind swelled into an enormous round dark hollow, and all about the roundness there were sudden bright flashes of light, trickling sweat, the abrasive texture of the towel, flies.

Marion studied him as he lay asleep. In the sunlit heat, it seemed to her hours passed. Asleep, he appeared to her more exposed than she had ever before seen him, his body oiled with sweat. She watched the sweat roll across his forehead and down his temples. A thin stream of sweat appeared to well up from his navel and trickle into his groin. His legs separated and his right hand went to his groin to pull at his scrotum with a finger. His genitals dripped sweat. She saw, as if it were slightly startled, his glans contract then swell a little.

She thought : if she touched him, she would be lost.

She stretched; she tried to yawn.

His body glowed. She sensed an odorous heat beam off it. He made small jerking gestures with his hands, his legs and feet kept shifting their positions, his torso rocked slightly from side to side as did his head, his lips, nostrils, eyelids moving. Her tight arm, as if the compulsion were in her bones, tried to reach out and stroke him across his chest; his skin would be alive with heat. She rubbed her kneecap. She kept both her arms close to her. She got up when the compulsion rose in her with a kind of physical recklessness to slap him suddenly. She turned away.

She was giddy. She walked into the sunlight, over the rocks. She picked up a dry stick and beat the rocks. Now and then she looked towards Valerian and each time her giddiness increased. She approached him, dragging the stick, and her giddiness, widened into an almost irrepressible recklessness, as though she were drunk, and knew she were drunk, and knew she couldn't do anything about it, made her raise the stick to strike him with it. She was startled, but her recklessness, she knew, would make her do anything. She dropped the stick when she saw him shake his head and sit up.

He saw Marion standing, her back to him.

He asked, but it was as if he were still asleep. 'Will you go in swimming?'

She looked around at him. 'I can't bear the sunlight any longer.'

He rose. 'I'll come in with you.'

They had to put on their sandals to walk to a crevice in the rocks down which they reached the sea. They descended by stepping on protrusions of stone that formed irregular steps. At the bottom of the cleft they took off their sandals, placed them out of reach of breaking waves, and stepped out on to a large flat slab of stone covered with yellow and orange algae, soft and wet beneath their feet, that rose up like grass in a strong wind when waves swept over it. Marion bent to look into a rock pool, where, among limpets, bluish chrysalis-like shrimps, old hermit-crab shells, the long delicate growths of pale-green seaweeds, two closed sea anemones stuck to the rocks – two huge semi-transparent red blood corpuscles.

She stood. She went to the edge of the stone slab and, poising herself only for a second, she dived in, but the second was held in his mind, and even after she had disappeared he saw her streaked hair, her smooth back, her buttocks, her thighs, the calves of her legs, her full body against the profoundly blue sea. She surfaced and swam out of the narrow view the steep cleft allowed.

He sat on the rock. The waves crashed over his legs, sometimes reached his waist, and buffeted him so he kept slipping on the algae.

It seemed to him he still saw the image of Marion poised at the edge of the rock, and in his mind he all at once saw radiating from it the infinite possibilities of his reaching her, of his pressing in on her with enough evidence of his love for her that she would not be able to deflect it. The infinite possibilities! He closed his eyes. It was just because there were so many possibilities that he could not reach her. She was protected – if to be protected was what she tried for – not by her own distance, but by his inability to reach her in any particular way, his inability to select the one word, the one expression, which would touch her. He opened his eyes. He saw the black sky, the blue-black sea. But then, he thought, he did not want to reach her in any particular way, did not want to touch but a part of her. No. He wanted to press on her in all ways, simultaneously, with the pressure of the very infinitude that made it impossible for him to ever feel he was in direct contact with her. He was never in direct contact with her. That didn't upset him. What upset him, what obsessed him, was to make the possibilities, however indirect, complete enough to surround her, exhaustive enough to exhaust her, rich enough to hold her, passionate enough to defy her repudiation. He could not be direct with her – he knew that deeply – but he could encircle her with arrows whose indirectness she would never be able to ward off. One day they would, all together, plunge in her, and she would change –

He stood.

He took three leaping strides to the edge of the rock and dived off. The blinding crash through the water stunned him. The impetus of the plunge forced him deep, and he gave in to it till it left him suspended below, and he rose slowly to the surface, which he saw shimmering above him like a strange, white, undulating sky. He burst through it, swept his hair back with his hands, breathed in deeply, and submerged. He saw, far below him, dark ravines and caverns, enormous fallen slabs of the coast, great boulders, a vast landscape softly illuminated by the light slanting through the blue-green water, and he was not swimming, but flying above it, flying across its sky in loose, slow, easy motions and twists of his naked body. Where the sea broke against the urchin-studded rocks that rose up into the coast there were vast, billowing, underwater clouds. He rose to breathe, then sank again. Beneath him, a school of small, royal-blue, iridescent fish swam past. He sank lower. The fish darted in all directions. He somersaulted. He rubbed his body. He rose, then sank again.

He continued to feel that he was flying through great aqueous spaces. When he saw, at a vague green distance, a body floating in the space, he flew towards it. In slow motion, he flew above a bare, steep mountain, and found Marion suspended over a wide canyon so deep she couldn't see the bottom of it. He thought that if he didn't get to her quickly she would fall into it, and with a sudden fear of falling himself, he swam more quickly, surfacing at times for breath. Her hair was all out, and her body was green. She made some signs, pointing down, but he could not make out what she meant. They both surfaced.

The atmosphere above seemed too thin, their gestures of throwing back their hair too rapid. Valerian asked:

'What were you pointing at?'

'The valley beneath us.'

She sank. He followed her. They swam towards the coast, she ahead so he could watch her, her protracted motions, her legs slowly kicking, her arms going in and out, in and out, her whole body dappled green, blue, at times yellow and rose. It came to him suddenly that he had just come across her in this dense sky, and he was letting her draw him along behind her.

She took him into an inlet that narrowed then widened into

a pool. At the end of the pool was a high arched entrance to a sea cave. They trod water.

She said, 'Follow me.'

She smiled, turned from him, and continued swimming.

Underwater, he saw her gliding forward to the entrance. She disappeared. When he approached he realized she had passed into the deep shadow of the cave, where the water turned very cold. He swam quickly, looking for her.

Up ahead there was light. He lifted his head from the water and saw that the roof at the back of the cave had fallen in, and brilliant sunlight streamed down, illuminating high smooth rocks that were blood-red, imperial purple, mauve. The water swelled and fell, swelled and fell. Valerian took a deep breath and dived under, and beneath saw, magnified through indigo-blue water that ran ultramarine in currents, the bases of those high rocks, as smooth as pebbles, which were redder, more deeply purple, more delicately mauve below, tinged with yellow and orange. Around them swam royal-blue fish and other fish striped in bands of blue and green and rusty red. He swam closer to the rocks. Avoiding the clusters of spiky urchins, he rose to the surface, but kept in contact with the rocks; his body floating out, he slowly manoeuvred his way around them, and on the other side of a large rock he found Marion sitting on a low round boulder, her body gleaming. She stood, stretched herself high in the awareness that he was watching her from below, and with a startling leap towards him, she dived in.

He felt her skim past him. Just as he turned, he felt her again, gliding across his back, and then he felt her hand across his chest and stomach. He submerged also and saw her swimming rapidly towards him. She glanced off him. Her thigh rubbed against his. He darted for her, but she quickly swam behind a rock. He followed. She wasn't there. He saw, just behind another rock, a foot kick, then disappear, and he went quickly. He caught her by the ankle. They surfaced. Valerian let go, and Marion again dived under and disappeared, but a moment later he heard laughter, bright and rich, echoing in the high, dripping cave.

Her continuing recklessness urging her, she swam deeper into the cave, as though deeper into a throat, where she clambered over boulders, beyond which the ground was too steep for the water to reach, and the roof of the cave was low enough to touch. The air was damp and cold. About her were plastic bottles and cups and the arms and legs of rubber dolls, all the flotsam smeared with oil. She went in deeper, squeezing between boulders, and found herself in a little chamber where the air was dense with dampness and the smells of salt, seaweed, rotting fish. The walls were rough, and black insects crawled over them in millions. On the floor was a thickness of weeds. She felt deeply closed in, felt that a part of the roof might suddenly fall in and she would not be able to get out; but she didn't leave.

She thought: she must get out, she would catch cold. She rubbed her arms and looked attentively at the swarms of insects on the walls. She imagined them swarming over her, and that made a shiver run through her, but she stayed.

A moment later Valerian came in. His wet body appeared to have a blue cast, as if the heavy air were permeated with phosphorus, as if they were still underwater and were able to remain there. The chamber was small. They stood close together. Valerian said nothing, but, his face expressionless, he came very near her and put his wet hands on her shoulders, then pressed her to him. She felt his wet chest, his stomach, his cock, his legs. He didn't kiss her, but just held her, then let her go, taking hold of one hand to bring her out of the chamber. But she held back.

He turned round to her. She wouldn't go, and wouldn't let go of his hand. She looked at him, and, as if all her recklessness broke into her taking a great and sudden risk, she drew him towards her, sensing pass between them as he stepped to her a great rush of what she knew love-making would only make a desperate attempt to express, no matter how wild the love-making. She reached out and touched the middle of his chest. Then, suddenly, she knew that if she did more there would follow an uncontrollable reaction, not from him, but from her. She pulled her hand away. There was a knock in the middle of her chest. She pressed her hand to it. She looked about. She didn't know where she was.

She had to get out quickly into the sunlight.

She retained the sense of not knowing where she was, not even in terms of longitudes and latitudes, as they bicycled back over the bumpy dirt roads, between the stone walls, over which grew tangles of thorny blackberry vines that appeared shrivelled and black, as if a fire had swept through them.

She pedalled fast, leaving him behind, and arrived at the house before him. She leaned the bicycle against the house and went in. She was panting and sweating. The house was cool. In the kitchen she drank down a half-bottle of cold mineral water. She threw off her clothes, ran into the bathroom and splashed cold water over herself, then hurried, her wet foot-marks left on the floor, to the bedroom. It was dim and cool, though bright light streaked through the slats of the shutters and across the bed. She threw herself down on the bed and circled her fingers about her face.

She heard Valerian come in. She heard running water. She heard his wet footsteps slapping the tiles. He came into the bedroom. She lay still. He lay down beside her. She didn't move, but through the spaces between her fingers she could see him, naked also, sipping a glass of mineral water, which he placed at different points against his chest. He put it on the floor. He lay back, his hands under his head. His eyes were open. She could see him breathing. Her own breath was hot against her face. She pressed her forehead deep into the pillow and clasped her hands closer about her face. Then, with a sudden jolting leap of all her body, she clutched at him.

When they rose, the streaks of light had moved up to the ceiling, and were fading into bands of violet. They staggered a little, and Marion had to sit back on the edge of the bed again before she could stand upright. She looked up at Valerian, who, leaning against the wall, was pressing with a finger of his left hand the yellow, black and blue patch which had appeared about the red circle of deep teeth marks on the fleshy underpart of his right forearm.

She fell back on to the bed. She turned away from him, but he surrounded her still, as though his body had been minutely dismembered and the parts – lips, nostrils, the lobes of his ears, the back of his neck, his elbows, fingers, ankles, toes – were raging about her, and she could not make any sense of them, could not bring them all together in one body which, together, she would be able to see for what it starkly was. She saw herself grasping an ear, a wrist, an arm.

Surprising even herself, she jumped up and suddenly held on to Valerian, still standing against the wall, to press herself to him as she would press herself against a hard surface; but, pressed against him, she thought she would explode.

She pulled away from him. Valerian left the room. Marion opened the shutters and leaned out.

The bruise on his arm burned. Valerian kept spreading spit over it. In the darkness, no one could see him; he walked about the garden, where the dry daisy stalks cracked as he passed through them. He should get back to Marion, he thought; he shouldn't leave her alone. But he himself, he realized, had to be alone.

When he went into the house he found her, dressed, washing a fish in the kitchen. He sensed the great tenseness of her calm.

She lay in the bathtub. Valerian stood before the basin, shaving.

She asked quietly for the soap.

Just as she grasped it before he let go, she felt she shouldn't take it. The water splashed over the side of the tub when she dropped it.

Valerian looked around to her. He asked, 'Are you all right?'

'Yes,' she said.

In the bedroom, she picked up one of Valerian's socks from the floor and stared at it.

Marion walked on ahead and turned to see Valerian, stopped, picking berries. She continued.

She felt she had to move carefully, as she was not sure what her body would do if she took a step that jolted her. She stopped. She looked back at Valerian again, whose body appeared to her to pulse, and, almost as she had come to expect it to happen, but not with such force, she felt, from inside, that she was being knocked in many different directions, knocked at from just beneath her lungs, with great deep thumps that made it difficult for her to breathe, that made her weak. She had to sit in the dirt road. She must stop this, she thought, she must. She would not let it get the better of her. She would resist it, she would fight it, she would break it.

Valerian came quickly to help her get to her feet. She hit him with the side of her arm to get him away from her.

'What's wrong?' he asked.

'Let me be!' she said. 'Let me be!'

She got up. They walked on. Marion breathed with difficulty, and felt, still, that all her insides were being stretched. No, she thought, no. She would not let it happen. She was not going to be broken. Valerian was not going to break her. She tried to concentrate: she would break him.

Marion sat at the stern of the little boat looking down at the rusted tin used for bailing. She didn't raise her head. She said, 'I mean your friend.'

'Ronald?'

'Yes.'

'I thought you wouldn't even recall him.'

'I recall him.'

'He won't come,' Valerian said.

'Ask him.'

'But why? You won't get along.'

'I want him to be here.'

Both stood on the quai.

The boat pulled into the port. Ronald Ghee watched the high land, the houses, the trees, the zigzagging road up the side of the coast appear to enlarge as if a telescope were swiftly bringing them all into greater focus. He saw Marion on the quai, looking away from the boat to a risen, docked submarine; a coil of rope was at her feet. Ronald swept the port for Valerian. He found him standing by a tree, his arms crossed, looking down at his feet with which he was scuffing the cement as to kick away a bit of tar or an oil stain. Then Valerian turned to find Marion. He walked across the cracked cement quai to her, they spoke, Marion shook her head, and Valerian looked away.

The guide ropes pulled taut. The boat bumped against the rotting beams of wood along the dock. Valerian and Marion were almost directly below Ronald, but they still didn't look up. As the gangplank was brought up, however, Valerian peered up to see the deck, and Ronald, wondering why he did, looked away to give Valerian the impression that he hadn't noticed him and Marion. When, finally, he looked down, both Valerian and Marion, their hands shading their eyes, were looking up at him.

They stood just to the side of the stream of disembarking passengers. Ronald put his valise to the ground. There was a space of no more than two feet between them and him, but, seeing their eyes close to, it came over him with a slight sensation of cold that the space was in fact enormous, and he immediately realized that he shouldn't have come, should have ignored Valerian's invitation. The sensed space between him and them was extended into a long time passing, though it could have only been a momentary hesitation. It was long enough, though, for Ronald to quickly decide that he would not be the first to react, would not take any initiative; it would all have to come from Valerian. As though he were leaping across the space, Valerian all at once embraced him with a sudden tight clinch and released him. He smiled largely, and reaching down for Ronald's valise said, 'We thought you might not come.'

'I would have let you know if I weren't,' he said, puzzled. He looked at Marion.

She was smiling in a way that made Ronald think she didn't quite know how to smile.

'The post is very bad,' she said.

The other passengers had gone, or were waiting for taxis. The three friends stood together. Again, Ronald thought: he would do nothing, would start nothing; they'd stand as they were until Valerian moved. But then, glancing at Valerian, whose smile was deliberately sustained, the heavy valise pulling down his arm and shoulder, he saw that he was waiting for him to greet Marion. Ronald turned towards her. The sunlight was full on her face; it exposed thin wrinkles about her eyes, a mole on her jaw, a curling black hair on her upper lip, and he saw in her eyes a startling, sunlit blankness. He didn't know how to approach her. He held out his hand to her. He saw her look down to it, and he let his hand drop. He said, 'Hello, Marion.'

She tried to straighten her smile.

Valerian hefted the valise. 'We'll have to wait for a taxi,' he said.

Outside the town, the taxi turned off on to a dirt road over which it rattled so much that Ronald imagined it rattling apart, leaving them sitting in the midst of a dry, flat landscape.

He wanted to be alone with Valerian.

Valerian, holding Marion's hand, showed him around the house. Ronald's room, in which the three stood uncertainly, had blank walls, a door that opened on to an empty terrace, windows that gave out to views of long low stretches of grey-brown countryside with diminishing perspectives of stone walls.

Marion sat at the edge of his bed; he had thought she would leave as quickly as possible to stay away from him. The talk, between Ronald and Valerian, kept shifting, was dropped, was started on a different subject, and Ronald wondered if it was the presence of Marion that made it so general, so unsettled. After a while she got up from the bed and went to the window to look out; Ronald saw, below her, a mass of cacti. His talk with Valerian stopped.

Valerian said to her, 'Shall we go rest?'

She smiled, not at Valerian, but at Ronald; he did not know what to make of the smile. 'No,' she said.

'I think perhaps we should.'

'If you want to rest,' she said to Valerian, 'go. I'm not tired.'

'You were a couple of hours ago.'

'Yes. But now I'm not.'

Valerian approached her. Ronald noted that she immediately drew away from the window and stood near the wall.

'Maybe Ronald wants to rest,' he said.

Marion looked at Ronald. 'Do you? Are you tired?'

'Oh, I slept well on the boat,' Ronald said.

Marion turned to Valerian. 'You go.'

'You come with me.'

She again looked at Ronald, and again smiled. 'You don't want him to go now, do you? Wouldn't you like to talk?' She took a few steps towards the door. 'Perhaps I should leave you both to talk.'

Valerian stepped up to her. 'That doesn't matter.' He didn't look at Ronald. 'Don't leave us.'

'For a little,' she said.

'No, not now.'

She said to him, 'But he's come a long way to see you.' She paused; she closed her eyes for a moment, then opened them, and said, 'Perhaps I am tired.'

'Then we'll go and rest.'

'Stay with him,' she said, 'stay with your friend.'

Valerian took her by the arm. He said to Ronald, 'She must rest.'

Ronald wanted to ask why she couldn't rest by herself. He was left alone in the bare room.

He went downstairs quietly and stepped outside. The sunlight fell like stones. Hunching his shoulders, he went further out, into the garden, where nothing grew but great cacti on the fleshy lobes of which prickly pears were blossoming. Where there was no cactus, there were stalks of dry daisies.

He stopped by a shuttered window. From inside, he heard Valerian saying, 'Oh, oh,' in a voice that sent a needle-like sensation over Ronald's back and shoulders, and with the sensation came the realization that whatever was going on between Valerian and Marion he didn't want to know about it; it would be better for him not to know about it; all he wanted to do was to draw Valerian away from it. He wanted to get Valerian by himself; he wanted, with a desire that would enclose them both, to take Valerian in his own arms. No, he thought, it was not even just a question of wanting; he must.

He continued, silently, avoiding the dry daisy stalks. He came to the kitchen garden, long dry furrows of earth where a few stunted tomato plants grew. Two of the plants, reduced to stalks, were entirely covered with snails. He circled the house, entered, and wondered what he should do.

The whole house, now, was silent.

At dinner, he felt it was only his presence which kept Valerian and Marion still and quiet, because they were, with him, very still, very quiet, as though they were holding themselves back from what would, if they gave in to it, separate them from him even more than their quiet and stillness did. He at times wondered if, when he spoke to them, they heard him.

He couldn't sleep. All night he thought he heard voices from downstairs.

In the morning, he saw in their faces that Valerian and Marion had not slept either. From the sitting-room, where they had coffee and bread, he saw through their open bedroom door their bed, the sheets in a twisted tangle. Valerian, catching him looking in, got up as to get more bread and, passing the door, shut it.

Marion said, 'We should go out today. We should go on an excursion.'

Valerian asked, 'You want to?'

She said, 'I don't want to stay in.'

Valerian said to Ronald, 'This must be because you're here.'

Ronald tried to laugh. 'No. I'm staying out of it.'

Marion said, 'Won't you come?'

'I think you and Valerian should go off on your own.'

'Oh no,' she said quickly, 'you must come.'

He went reluctantly. They hired a car. Ronald drove to a spot where, as indicated by a black dot on the map, there were prehistoric dwellings in the side of a cliff. They drove through farms, and thin wiry dogs, whose right forelegs and right back legs were chained together, limped after the car, barking shrilly. They couldn't find the caves, and tried to figure out just where they were on the map.

Valerian said, 'Obviously the map is wrong.'

'It can't be,' Ronald said.

'It is,' he insisted.

Ronald studied it again. 'I think we should turn off at our next left,' he said, and put the car into gear.

The next left was a track overgrown with dry weeds. Ronald eased the car on to it.

'You won't find it,' Valerian said.

'I will,' Ronald said.

The car bounced deeply over the jutting rocks and ruts. The dry weeds brushed and cracked under the car. The windshield was covered with fine dust, and dust billowed in through the windows. Ahead, Ronald saw a ridge, like an eroded shoulder-blade, rise at the far side of a bare field.

'That must be it,' he said.

They left the car and walked across the field.

Marion stayed near Ronald, Valerian close behind. They crossed a wide patch of sand, like a small desert. Their shoes sank in and the heat penetrated the leather. At the other side of the patch was a cliff face, high up on which were regular openings, like doorways.

Valerian immediately searched for a way up to one of the entrances. He found a steep narrow ridge, and, holding on to jutting bits of stone, started up. Ronald came up behind him.

Marion said, 'Don't go.'

Ronald turned back. He was not sure whom she had spoken to.

'Don't go,' she repeated.

He pointed to himself. 'Shouldn't I see as well?'

'It'll only be a big hole in the rock,' she said.

He stepped down. Valerian was climbing, stepping uncertainly, pausing now and then to get a firm foothold. Ronald and Marion watched him.

'Let's go back to the car,' Marion said. Her face was shining with perspiration.

'And leave him?'

They looked up at Valerian again. He was approaching an entrance. Marion's voice sounded urgent:

'Let's go.'

Valerian stopped outside the entrance and looked down. There was a sheer drop just below him.

'Aren't you coming up?' he called, and, again, Ronald wasn't sure whom he was addressing, but he felt it was he.

'Watch out or you'll fall,' he said.

'Come on,' Valerian called down.

Ronald was suddenly sweating profusely; it seemed to him it was the presence of Marion that made him.

'Come on,' Valerian repeated. 'It's not difficult.'

Ronald pretended he didn't hear him. Avoiding turning towards Marion, he stepped around a mass of stony rubble that had fallen from the cliff side. He glanced up at Valerian, who was hurrying down.

Marion walked quickly, Ronald by her. As though the words had been considered for a long time, she said, 'You and Valerian are close, aren't you?'

It was almost as if he were defying her. 'Yes.' Then he took a mental step backward. 'We were.'

'No more?'

'That's up to him.'

'Try to get him alone. Try to talk to him.'

'About what?'

'About yourselves. Remind him that you were close.'

'Why?' he asked sharply.

'He needs someone to help him.'

He paused. 'Yes.'

It seemed to him there was much more she had wanted to say to him, but all of it moved, he sensed, in different directions in her head, and it occurred to him how difficult it must have been for her to say anything.

The three sat on piles of seaweed in a deserted cove where Valerian was finally talking to him, Ronald thought, though what they talked about had nothing to do with why he had come such a long way to be with him. Marion, not listening, it seemed, disentangled shells from the seaweed.

She suddenly got to her feet and started to walk off.

'Where are you going?' Valerian asked.

She glanced at Ronald as if for assistance, then said to Valerian, 'Please let me go off; please let me be by myself.'

'Let her go,' Ronald said.

Valerian was about to get up, but, rising, he looked at Ronald, who held him with a stare; Valerian seemed confused. He sat back.

Ronald tried to hold Valerian down with his stare, but as Marion went off Ronald saw come over Valerian's face as he watched her cross the beach and disappear among the rocks a look as of knowing all at once that she wouldn't return; it was a look of such simplicity that Ronald wondered what state Valerian was in to not be able to see the simplicity and detach himself from it. The look startled Ronald, and it took him a while to assert, to himself and for Valerian, that of course he could get out of his state; he would survive, because people did survive one another. He said:

'Will you stay here long?'

Valerian turned towards him. 'On the island?'

'Yes.'

'As long as we need,' Valerian said.

'For what?'

Valerian didn't continue. He rose to his feet and started towards the rocks. Ronald rose also.

'Let her be,' Ronald said.

'You don't know. She may do something to herself.'

'She can't do any more to herself than what you're doing.'

'And what am I doing?'

Ronald grabbed him by the arm. 'Leave her alone. Stay with me. We've hardly spoken since I arrived. You asked me to come here, you owe me at least the little consideration of speaking to me by yourself.' He pushed down on Valerian's shoulder, pressing him to sit on the sand, and he sat beside him.

Alone with him, Ronald tried to pick up the familiar talk, knowing it was not what he wanted, then he fell silent. After a while he gave up and went into the sea.

He swam out slowly to a rock and climbed up on it. He could see the whole cove, the white strip of the beach, and Valerian sitting on it as he had left him.

He saw Marion emerge from the twisted, sea-corroded rocks. She stood back, a small figure on the sweep of the beach. She half turned, and it appeared to Ronald that she was about to go among the rocks again, but Valerian saw her, and, jumping up, went towards her. Perhaps she said something to stop him, but Ronald couldn't hear. Valerian took a few steps backwards. Marion walked in a wide semi-circle around him to the centre of the beach, where she appeared to look for something – maybe for Ronald himself. Valerian approached her, and she moved to the side, nearer the sea, and at the edge of the sea stopped; Valerian, too, stopped, still a long distance from her, then, after a moment, he moved to the side, towards a great heap of seaweed, and as he moved away, Marion moved forward, and they crossed one another. They faced one another, then, it seemed, exchanged places, circled one another in wide arcs, stopped, reversed their steps, stopped, drew further apart, then advanced towards one another and passed one another, as if they were, on the beach, performing a slow complex dance whose pattern Ronald couldn't figure.

He felt he was witnessing something he had no right to be seeing. He looked out towards the sea.

They had dinner outside under a vine. Beetles fell from the vine on to the table and the stone paving beneath. As Ronald left them to go to his room, he paused momentarily inside the door and heard, through Valerian and Marion's silence, the beetles falling.

He undressed and lay on the bed.

Lying still, he thought of Valerian as he had known him. He imagined the room he was in, and all the rooms in the house, enormous, the ceilings high and in shadows, the walls wide and blank, and everything there was between him and Valerian diminished by the space. Perhaps all there was between them, really, was familiarity. He had loved Valerian because he had known Valerian.

He found Marion standing at the open door of the hall as he came downstairs. She was leaning against the door jamb, looking out. The morning light blazed around her. She turned to him.

'It's hot again today,' she said.

'Will it cool?'

'No.' She was barefoot. She walked across the tiles to the sitting-room and Ronald followed her. She sat, and he did.

'Where is Valerian?' Ronald asked.

'He's gone out.'

'Where?'

'For milk, I think.'

'He should have waited. I would have gone with him.'

'He wouldn't have let you go with him.'

'Why?'

'He doesn't want to be alone with you.'

'Why doesn't he?'

'He's afraid you'll try to make him go back.'

'I want him to come back.'

'Ah!'

He saw tears come to her eyes.

'You see, don't you, that you can't continue,' he said.

'I see,' she said.

'Will you help me?' he asked.

She passed her hand across her forehead. 'There's nothing I can do.'

'You can't leave him?'

'Oh, I! Let's not think about me. I don't want anyone to think about me. Think about him. Get him away from me. Take him away with you.'

She stopped. Valerian was standing at the door, a milk pail in one hand. He looked to Ronald to be wan, but perhaps it was the bright white light.

Marion got up quickly and went into the bedroom; Ronald stopped Valerian in the middle of the floor from following her.

Ronald said, his voice high, 'Listen to me!'

Valerian's eyes, fixed on Ronald, were large with sudden anger; he said nothing.

'You won't succeed,' Ronald said, 'you know you won't succeed.'

'And what do you think I will do?' Valerian asked, his voice pitched higher than Ronald's.

Ronald's voice was empty and flat. 'You won't do anything.'

All the expression went out of Valerian's face.

'You've done nothing,' Ronald insisted, 'and you know you won't do anything. It's all been for nothing.'

Valerian left the house.

Ronald's sheets were damp and stuck to him as he turned over. In the darkness of the room, he could see the grey rectangles of the open windows and doorway which gave out to the terrace. Then he heard movement. He rose up on his elbows.

'Who is it?' he asked.

There was no answer; he saw a figure step into the grey rectangle of a window.

'Who is it?' he asked again, and Valerian's voice said his name, 'Ronald,' and his shoulder jumped with the touch of Valerian's hand. He moved away when Valerian sat on the edge of the bed. Ronald asked, 'What do you want?'

The tone of Valerian's voice was deep, was conciliatory. 'If I could tell you what, really, I want –'

Ronald felt as if thousands of tiny sharp wires were snapped all over his body. 'I'd give it to you,' he said.

He heard Valerian's deep breathing. 'You couldn't.'

'I can. I know what you want.'

'You don't. You don't. I want you to leave.'

Ronald paused. 'Then why did you want me to come?'

'I didn't,' Valerian answered.

'You didn't?'

'No. Marion wanted you to come. She asked me to ask you.'

'Why?'

'She insisted on it, desperately.'

'Desperately?'

'Yes. She thought that if you came, you would protect her; you would at least turn me away from her.'

'But why should she want you so desperately to leave her?'

'Because I love her.'

'Is that reason for her wanting you to go?'

'It is for her. She doesn't want to know what it means.'

'She wanted me to take you away?'

'Yes.'

'She still thinks it's possible, doesn't she?'

'No.'

There was a long silence. Ronald asked, 'Do you know what you're doing?'

'Yes.'

'What?'

'I'm losing touch,' Valerian said.

Ronald felt the thin wires beat wildly. 'And don't you care?'

'Yes, I care that I haven't lost even the slight touch I have left, that I haven't done away with all perspectives. I won't even be able to say her name finally, I'll be that incapable of seeing her from a perspective.'

'What will become of you?'

Valerian didn't answer.

'You don't know?' Ronald asked.

'No.'

'You'll go all the way?'

'Yes.'

'Do you know what risk you're taking?'

Again, Valerian said nothing.

Ronald said, 'That no one, no one at all, will follow you – not because they can't, not because it's impossibly difficult, but because they simply won't care.'

Valerian was silent.

'I, certainly, won't follow,' Ronald said.

The silence fell deeper.

Ronald suddenly said, 'Val, leave her. We can go back together.'

Valerian put his arms around Ronald, who stayed rigid for a moment, then held Valerian, and the two men's breathing rose and fell. Then, slowly, Valerian let go as though a number of tendons, one after another, gave way, and Valerian fell away from Ronald and lay full length across the bed.

Valerian was still for a moment, then he got up and went out.

At dawn, Ronald found Marion outside. She was standing by a tree; the branches moved in a hot wind; his quiet approach startled her.

He said, 'You wanted to be alone.'

She smiled.

'Valerian is still alseep?'

'Yes.'

He looked up. 'It's strange to see a totally empty sky with a wind blowing; the wind seems to come from nowhere.' He paused. "I'll be leaving today.'

'I thought you might.'

'Did Valerian say that I would?'

'No. I felt you'd go.'

'He doesn't want me.'

She asked him, 'Did he love you?'

He didn't answer.

She turned away, but asked, 'Will he let me be?'

'No,' Ronald said.

After he saw Ronald off, Valerian walked up into the town. The shops were closing. Someone had dropped a basketful of tomatoes; they lay squashed, thick patches of red, on the cobbles. In the market square, more squashed vegetables and fruit lay about. An old woman was rummaging through a pile of garbage. The high narrow streets took him to the top of the town, where, on a wide dusty square across which a strong wind blew, he sat at a café. It was a long while before a waiter came over and when he did Valerian wasn't sure what he wanted; he ordered a lemonade and immediately regretted it, for he saw a man at another table drinking an aperitif and he wished he had ordered one himself. But it was too much bother to change the order. It was too much bother, he thought, to do anything but give in to what happened. There was nothing he could do but give in, because with Ronald had gone any pretence he might have had to determine anything, to keep Marion within any bounds that would allow him to deal with her. He got his lemonade. It wasn't what he wanted. He had wanted a freshly squeezed lemon. This drink came from a bottle, and fizzed in his glass. It didn't matter.

He stood. He didn't want to return to Marion right away. For a short while, he wanted to be by himself.

He walked out of town, across a wide stretch of abandoned

farms, towards the sea. As he walked the wind blew harder, blowing dust, and the darkness fell deeper, making the sliver of a new moon appear like an incision in a vast black sheet on the other side of which an intense white light was beaming; the stars were pinpricks in the sheet.

He found a beach near what appeared to be a small refinery. Pale green lights flickered on the complicated buildings and chimneys. The beach was covered with litter and lumps of oil. The wind was blowing in from the sea. He went to the edge of the rising tide.

He picked up a bit of stone and squeezed it; the edges hurt his palm. His mind kept turning this way and that as if, like a telescope on a pivot, it were trying to find some distant point to focus on and establish the perspectives of some fixed decision. He realized his mind was doing this although it knew there was no decision to be made. It had already been made, and he could not now be sure it was he who had made it: it had been made in favour of putting his faith in everything he did not know. His mind spun around, and he knew it spun uselessly, but he couldn't stop it. He squeezed the rock more tightly.

He thought: if he were in a thinner atmosphere, the rock he held might melt away, and the sea might evaporate into a gas, and the air might cease to have any composition; or, if the atmosphere about him were very dense, the air might condense to a heavy liquid, the sea might draw together into a stony solid, and the stone he held – he looked at it – would so intensely draw in on itself, it would collapse in on itself, and all the laws that applied to it as he knew it now in his hand, wet and rough and covered with sand, would be suspended, so he couldn't even expect it to fall if he dropped it.

It was the so-taken-for-granted atmosphere as it was that allowed the stone its shape, but it seemed to him it would take so little to change all of that, some slight shift in the gravitational pull, some slight retuning of the music of the spheres, and everything, everything would change. He himself would change his shape. He could not bear the world as it was; he would do anything to make it change. He could not bear it because it was only what it was, and he wanted –

Oh, what he wanted! He wanted what gravity made impossible, what all the circles of the heavens, no matter how far one went, denied was possible. He imagined them now, like globes of decreasing size fitting into one another and turning in different directions, he imagined the great set atmosphere of the universe, then the atmosphere of the galaxy, then the atmosphere of the earth, then the atmosphere created by the palpable pull of people towards one another, and all the atmospheres were drawn together into creating what was so intolerably constant: what he knew about them all, what he knew about love, about hate, about friends and family, about eating and shitting and sleeping. Oh no, oh no, it was not this he wanted. He wanted an atmosphere where the laws of physics and biology and psychology made no sense, and where everything would be so different now it was unimaginable –

What his atmosphere was he didn't know, but he sensed it, sensed it so deeply the sense was itself a conviction of it, as he sensed, more strongly indrawing than anything he had ever sensed, the pull of Marion, someone in whom he knew everything he wanted was possible, in whom he would give way to a possessiveness, a mania, that would leave nothing of her untouched. She didn't know his resources, she didn't know how far he could go. He hadn't yet begun. He would exhaust her. He would go to the furthest limit of her, beyond the furthest limit, beyond laughing and crying, beyond thinking and feeling, to where relationships took on a depth and a passion which nothing known – not laughter, tears, kisses, blows – could express. He had this much faith in what he could do : he knew that he could love her with a love that was as transforming as death.

In her mind, Marion saw the two flies that circled her, enormous, with great hairy legs and phlegm-coloured wings. She realized she saw everything in her mind larger, in greater detail than she saw with her eyes open, as though her forehead were a thick curved glass through which the flies, the grains of sand, the spray of waves, the bottles and paper cups, the other people on the beach, were magnified. It was better to keep her eyes open, she thought, but that would mean staring up into the sunlight. She sat. At her side Valerian lay, his body wet, as he had just been in swimming. She noted the way his ribs showed more when he inhaled, the rising and sinking of his navel, the whiteness of his flesh about his armpits. She studied the hairs around his nipples, a cluster of three moles on his right shoulder. She closed her eyes.

She stood and went into the sea. The wind was strong, and so was the surf. The water was almost opaque with sand churned up from the bottom. A wave slapped against her, throwing her off balance. She sank and tried to swim under-water, but because of the sand she couldn't open her eyes, and her mind expanded the water around her into visions of the legs of swimmers kicking, sometimes kicking one another, of floating light-bulbs and lumps of oil, a twisting confusion of plastic bags. It seemed to her she would not be able to swim through the water, but would be tangled in and choked by arms and legs and debris. She went back to the shore.

She dropped on the sand, which stuck to her legs and got under her bathing suit. She pulled the wet cloth from her like a loose skin. She wished she could flay it off. She would not have had to wear it if she had not insisted they come to this beach, which was crowded. She wondered now why she had insisted. She moved her legs to let a little boy pass; he was carrying a large green sweating bottle of mineral water; his eyes were almost colourless, and he had a faint scar on his forehead. Marion shook her head to clear it of its attentiveness. She re-joined Valerian.

Beside him, she raked through the sand to find shells which she threw into a little heap. He turned on his side to look at her. She examined each shell she found: a tissue-paper-thin shell with rose smudges on it, a shell rough outside with variegations of green and pink inside, a thick rough shell covered with dark brown dots, another the colour and shape of a fingernail, another a snail shell. She must occupy her mind with something, she thought, but she couldn't bear the shells any more than she could bear the sight of the irises of Valerian's eyes, or his earlobes, or the streaks of sun-bleached hair – all these details, she thought, crowding around her. She buried the pile of shells.

She asked Valerian, 'Do you really want to stay here any longer?'

'You were the one who wanted to come,' he said.

She said, 'Yes, I know,' and realized she had wanted to come to be among people. 'Now I want to leave.'

'As soon as we get back to the house, you'll want to leave there as well.'

She stood. She walked to the edge of the water and back.

Valerian said, 'Perhaps we can make something in the sand.'

He picked up the towels, stuffed clothes and sandals into a duffel bag, and Marion followed him over a mass of rocks that jutted out into the sea. On the other side were boats pulled up on the little beach which was otherwise empty. The sand was wet. The wind made their hair blow.

Marion simply watched Valerian begin to scoop up handfuls of dripping sand and slap them on top of one another.

'Won't you help?' he asked.

'I don't know what you're making.'

'A woman,' he said.

She knelt down on the opposite side of the mound Valerian was making. They were, she thought, both fools. She piled up sand to make the outstretched legs and smoothed them out.

Valerian collected seaweed for the hair and shells for the eyes, nipples, navel. He was making a great effort to engage her, she saw, to bring all her growing restlessness together in making the sea-woman. But he had to fail, because the sea-woman herself made Marion restless for her lying so heavily still, for being so unaware she was made of nothing but dead

132

seaweed and shells and sand already cracking as the moisture drained out of it. Marion wanted to kick her apart.

It was difficult pedalling to the house. The wind blew against them. It was as though gravity were always pulling them back, and they had to push against it. They got off their bicycles to walk up the steepest hills.

Valerian walked ahead. In the dying light, Marion saw the muscles in the calves of his legs, saw his tangled hair blow, saw his shoulderblades move, saw the way his shorts rode with the sway of his hips, and she heard the cyclical *tic tic* of the ballbearings in his wheels. She could not take the sights, the sounds, any longer; she could not. They were like the constant flies, even now circling them, landing on her shoulders, neck, wherever she couldn't reach to swat them off.

By the time they had reached the house the sun had set.

Valerian prepared dinner. She was too tired, but she was unable to sit still. She tried to control herself by making herself sit for half an hour without moving; at the end of the half hour she thought she would burst. She went out. An ox-drawn cart was passing behind the low wall before the front garden, and the driver was singing; because of the bumps, his voice had an undulating wail to it. Marion went to the gate to watch the wagon disappear and listen to the voice cease. She thought: she must go away. But she turned away from the gate.

She must, at least, control herself in front of Valerian. She mustn't give him any indication that she was anything but always in control, even when she was most extreme. She wandered about the windy dry garden where the light of the full moon made all the details – the cactus thorns, the snail-encrusted branches, the dry heads of the daisies – visible, but visible, she thought, in a way that was unlike the visibility the sun gave; she was studying a geranium plant completely covered with snails when Valerian called her for dinner.

The moonlight grew brighter and cast violently moving shadows through the grape-vine on to the table. The light was so strong they didn't need candles. The wind grew, too, a hot wind from which they were protected by the garden wall. It shook the vine and made the spiky fronds of a palm tree in front of the house thrash one another.

Marion tried to keep still and silent all through the meal. Valerian kept filling her wine glass. The moonlight made the wine look black. Valerian brought out a melon and a knife.

The melon, too, looked black, round and full. He placed it on the table, the knife beside it, and picked up a dish which he was about to put before Marion. She picked up the knife and stabbed it into the melon, stabbed it again and again, until the rind cracked and juice ran out over the table. She put the knife down. She went into the house.

It was a long time afterwards that Valerian went into the bedroom to find her. If she was not sleeping, he thought, she was pretending to be, and he must let her alone.

He climbed the stairs to the room Ronald had used. The windows and door to the balcony were still open, and wind rushed through. Valerian lay on the bed. He heard shutters, loose glass, rusty hinges, slamming, shaking, creaking.

He fell asleep, or half fell asleep, and there were times when he woke, or perhaps dreamed that he woke, and heard voices and singing from far away. It seemed to him the space in the room kept changing, and his sweat-damp bed moved about. When he did really wake, the moonlight was brighter than he had ever known it to be. It flooded in through the windows and door. He got up and went out to the balcony.

The moon was enormous, a flesh colour, and the sky was a livid pink. The landscape below, cut across by rows and rows of stone walls, appeared in the light like no other landscape he had ever seen, and yet nothing in it had changed: the shuttered farmhouses were there, the stunted trees bending to the wind. He raised his hands and could see the lines on his palms.

He left the balcony and went downstairs. The noises the wind made were now clashing, and he could not believe

Marion was sleeping through them. He imagined her lying still, or trying to, listening.

In the garden, the dry stalks of daisies twisted and turned and the cacti shook. The white walls of the house appeared penetrated with the light, and his shadow moved against them. He did not know why he did, but he went across the garden to the shed, a kind of stone grotto, to look in; the tools, the burlap sacks, the piles of empty bottles were there, and he wondered if he had expected them not to have been. He noted, passing the cistern, that the water was absolutely clear all the way to the bottom. He returned to the house, but at the doorway stopped. He was frightened to go in, and he knew he would have to force himself to step into the bedroom where Marion was.

She was lying on her side with her knees drawn up and her arms clasping her legs. He approached her. He saw that she was trembling, trembling as with an exertion to hold on to something so tightly it would be crushed in her arms. He leaned over, he touched her elbow, and immediatley her body rearranged itself violently, so quickly he could hardly make out the motions. He drew back, and saw her now lying on her other side, facing away from him, her knees again raised up to her chest, her arms squeezing them. He stood back and watched her. A moment later there was another contortion of her body and then a knotting-up into a position that had her kneeling, her head low, her arms twisted under her.

He wondered if he should hold her, but he couldn't bring himself any closer to her, or touch her.

He saw a spasm go through her, saw her shoulders shudder, and he felt a shudder pass through himself, and pass again when, with a mechanical suddenness, she began to rock back and forth, hunched over on her knees.

Valerian said, 'Marion.'

If there was any response, it was only to rock faster.

'Please, Marion,' he said.

She stopped. He could hear her breathing heavily. He was

about to step towards her when her body, as though it were being picked up, was shaken, turned over and thrown about the bed, while the expression on her face was as of stunned awe at that was happening.

'Marion, stop it,' Valerian said.

She swung her arms about, and her legs thumped against the mattress.

'Stop it, please stop it.'

She would knock her head on the wall, he thought, or break her hand by cracking it against the headboard. And then she began to wail, a sound that came, it seemed to him, not from her, but from outside. He shut the windows.

His voice caught in his throat. 'Please stop it! Please stop it!'

Her body contorted again, and one arm extended across the mattress made jerky, repeated stabbing gestures.

Valerian said, 'Please! Stop! Stop!'

Then she was as though yanked from the position and again thrown about the bed. Her head bounced against the wall, but she didn't stop. Her hands were clenched, her toes stood out from one another as with cramp. Sweat poured from her, and the sheets and pillows were dragging on the floor. All the while she wailed, a high, high, wild sound.

'Please! Please stop it!'

In the midst of a grotesque, horrible dance, even while wailing, she sobbed: 'I can't. I can't stop.'

When, finally, he saw that she lay still, he quickly got away from her.

He propped his bicycle against a wall and went into the market, aware that whatever indefinite thing had happened to them, he had a strong enough sense of it to isolate it in his wonder: a sense, he thought, not an idea, because it couldn't be conceptualized; not a feeling either, because it left him feeling nothing. He could only wonder: it was like the gap he had in his mind when he was trying to recall a lost word or rhythm, or the hollow he had of an intention that hadn't found its expression, a gap that had no images and produced no feelings, and yet was there. That was the closest he could get to describing to himself the sense that preoccupied him : a gap that had not been in his mind before, and which now opened slit-like into a space before him. It seemed to him he saw everything through it, and the tomatoes, oranges, peaches, the plucked chickens hung upside down by their claws, the baskets of dried beans and chick-peas he passed by in the stalls of the market had about them something that escaped his attention; but the attention itself, with nothing definite to come to grips with, only increased the wonder of the sense he had. He knew he would not be able to grasp it, and even trying to grasp it would be like trying to make darkness visible, silence audible.

He bought what he had to buy, tied everything on to the carrier at the back of his bicycle, and set off. He was curiously detached.

On the way he stopped at a farm to pick up a covered pail he had left on the way to town to be filled with fresh milk. An old hunchbacked woman handed it to him over the gate. He hung the pail over the handle-bars. He heard the milk slosh.

When he got to the house, he found it empty. He went from room to room twice over. Still detached, that persistent gap keeping him calm, he searched the garden, the tool shed where her bike was, he went out to the dirt road to look, then came back into the house, went upstairs and out on to the balcony to look over the surrounding fields.

He put the groceries away before he got on to his bicycle again and pedalled into the village. The village consisted of twelve or so square, severe, white houses at a road crossing. There was only one shop, which sold bread and wine and soap, and where it was possible to buy cold drinks. He pushed aside the thin clinking chains over the doorway and went inside, but Marion wasn't there. He bought a cold tonic. He next went to the village fountain, a kind of stone walled alcove off one of the roads where there was a bench and shade from a tree. A man was sitting on the bench. He looked at Valerian, then turned away and spat. Valerian splashed water from the trough beneath the flowing spigot on to his face. The old man did not offend him. He took his time. When he left, it was as if he were on a leisurely ride, with no particular place to go. He rode to the centre of the village again, stopped in the middle of the X of the crossroads, and looked in all four directions. He pedalled off in the direction of the sea.

He had not before realized what a long ride it was, and yet, at the centre of his growing anxiety, there was that constant gap. He watched the front of the wheel bounce against the stones. Sometimes pebbles shot out from beneath the tyre. By concentrating on the point of ground just before the front wheel, the landscape appeared to streak past him, so he might have been going very fast; but he felt, too, that he wasn't moving at all, and the thought flashed in his mind that he should abandon the bicycle and run.

He threw the bike down on top of the sear rosemary bush by which they usually parked their bikes, and jumped across the rocks of the headland to the little beach they often went to. The soles of his sandals were smooth, and he was not able to get firm footholds on the uneven rock. He had to jump over a wide fissure; at the bottom of it was a pool of yellow water, like urine. He tottered when he landed, and thought for a second he would fall into the pool, but he was able to throw himself forward. He landed on his knees, on rock that looked like petrified sponge. One knee was bleeding. He hurried over the remaining headland, past the cavities lined with salt, to the little beach. He found the remains of a fire and a condom. He ran to the edge of the rocks to look over the sea.

Jumping over the rocks back to his bicycle, he wondered where else he should look, if he should contact the local police. He was thirsty and his bruised left kneecap had begun to pain, as though a bit of sharp stone had been embedded in it. He got on the bike and pedalled to the public beach they occasionally went to, which meant he had to retrace his way

138

across the wide dry fields, opening and closing gates as he went, until he reached the tarmac, which he must take down, down along the coast to the level of the sea where the headland gave way to a strip of beach. A few cars were parked on the sand, and beyond them were people sitting on canvas chairs. Valerian looked them over, as if Marion might be among them disguised; he went to the water's edge and searched the horizon.

His mouth was parched. He tried to bring moisture to it by sucking at the insides of his cheeks, but his panting as he pumped his way up the long hill kept his mouth open and dry. He couldn't make the steep parts of the incline. He walked up pushing his bicycle. He had to stop now and then to catch his breath.

He finally made it to a rubbish pile of gleaming bottles where he turned off the tarmac on to the dirt road. He pedalled as fast as he could, hardly able to avoid the big rocks. All he could do was pedal and hope the wheels would take the least resistant course. He felt his sweat flying off him. Just as, with a sensation of flying out, a sensation that seemed to him to last for ever, the bicycle sped over a rock that ended abruptly and left him in mid-air, it occurred to him that Marion hadn't taken her bicycle, she could not have gone far, and both the thought and the thump to the ground made him feel his stomach turn over. He was thrown off his seat and landed, sitting, on a stone, as if he had himself sat there just in time to watch his bike do a somersault with a kind of slow-motioned ease. He tried to collect himself : his buttocks were aching, he had snapped a strap on one sandal, and his kneecap kept bleeding. He rose carefully, righted the bicycle, and found the front tyre was flat.

He leaned the bicycle against one of the stone walls running along the road and sat where he had been, sat as though in a ring of fury that suddenly burst about him; it didn't touch him, he still felt detached, but he knew if he moved the flames would catch him, and the fury would take over. He was able to think: perhaps it wasn't detachment he felt, but a curious concentration, an empty concentration because nothing was yet subjected to it, and yet he could sense that whatever was finally subjected to it would be exploded by it. He mustn't move; he must be calm.

He rose, leaned for a moment on the handle-bars of his bicycle, then began to push it along the road. The sandal with the broken strap flapped; he had to walk with a peculiar step to keep it on. The flies settled on him, attracted by his sweat.

He was limping when he reached the house. He kept his movements slow and careful. He put the bicycle in the shed; the spokes of its front wheel tangled in twigs bundled for kindling, and he was about to jam the bike in anyhow and leave it, but he disentangled the twigs and lined up the bike next to Marion's. He walked very slowly into the house.

He found her sitting on the divan in the sitting-room. She was lying face down, one arm over the side, so her hand, curled into a loose fist, touched the floor. Valerian approached her quietly. It was only when he was standing above her that he saw she was breathing.

He knew then that if he had had a knife in his hand he would have killed her. He knew it, for in the middle of his exhaustion and aches and pains, his concentration was still calm, and he saw what he was capable of. She slowly turned over and looked at him. Her eyes narrowed and her lips were drawn in, making them thin and sharp. She sat up.

He sat on the edge of the divan. His voice startled him for its suddenness and loudness. 'Where were you?' She said nothing. She moved away from him. After a moment, she touched his arm, and he swung around and hit her as hard as he could.

She jumped up and ran to the other side of the room. She stood against the wall.

He saw that she saw he was terrified. She stood away from the wall to face him, standing up straight. She said, 'You don't know what you're doing.'

'No,' he said.

He wanted to kill her. It was like saying, 'It's hot, it's cold.' He did not quite know what it meant, but he knew it was there, like the weather, and it did not seem to him to have anything to do with him.

He waited outside the house for her. His white shirt shone into the darkness around him. He walked back and forth in front of the door. He didn't hear her come out. He turned around and found her standing in the doorway. She was wearing a dress and her hair was carefully done up. He let her go first through the garden and closed the gate after them.

They walked silently. People were hurrying past them to the village, from where music echoed over loudspeakers, interrupted now and then by an amplified voice. They had to move to the side of the road occasionally to let a car or a rusty pick-up truck or an ox-drawn cart pass. At the back of one cart sat, in a row, five children, three boys and two little girls, their bare feet dangling, their eyes very wide, each one carrying a flower; they stared at Valerian and Marion as they passed as if they could not believe that people from outside the village and the surrounding farms existed.

Valerian noted other people turning to look at them as they approached the crossroads of the village where lights had been strung up from house to house.

He held back, and Marion did also. She was staring straight ahead. He imagined her standing in a crowd formed in a thick circle around her, and she stood in a space that none of the men in the crowd – they were all men – would step into, though they pressed closer and closer to it, and from which they wouldn't let her leave. They held her there, surrounding her, isolating her, while something in them checked them from hedging any nearer to her.

Marion paused to take a pebble out of one of her shoes. She leaned against a stone wall to do it. She was, it seemed to

Valerian, utterly defenceless in being so exposed to the people who of course watched her. He stood closer to her to hide her, and as he did he realized he, too, watched her in the same way, surrounded her in the same way a crowd would. She put her shoe back on, and they continued. Valerian kept staring at the people around to deflect their stares from Marion, but he couldn't do it; they stared right through him.

He looked at Marion, then down the road to the village, then looked at her again, at her large dark unblinking eyes, and in them images of her dead came to him. All at once there broke in him feelings which made him reach out and take her arm and draw her near him.

'Would you like to go back to the house?' he asked.

'Would you?' she asked in return.

He shook his head. 'I want to do what you want.'

But he could see that she did not know what she wanted. She searched the gathering crowd as to find someone who would make up her mind for her. Valerian said quickly:

'Never mind. We'll look around, then go back.' He added: 'Please tell me if you're tired.'

She nodded.

He thought: she was a child. He drew her closer to him, recognizing the feelings he had had a moment before: of a pity so intense he had to restrain himself from putting his arms around her and holding her.

Close to her, he noticed a scar on her jaw where it curved up under her ear. It was the first time he had noticed it. He realized he knew nothing about her, and that now he wanted to ask, 'Where did you get that scar?' He did ask, and touched the spot.

Her own hand jumped to touch it. Their hands collided. She frowned.

'A scar?' she asked.

'Yes.'

'No doubt when I was young.'

'A little girl?'

'Yes, a little girl.' She frowned more. 'Before I started school, I think.'

'You're not sure?'

'No.' She paused. 'No, I'm not sure.'

Valerian waited.

'Perhaps it happened once when I climbed a tree.'

'When you were so little?'

'I wonder now if there was someone to hoist me, but I don't think so. I think I was alone. Perhaps it was an apple tree, and there was a ladder against it for picking the apples, and I climbed up, then stepped on to a branch, and up into higher ones.'

'Were you hiding from someone?'

'No. I just climbed up, but once I got up I was frightened because I didn't know how to get down. I could see the crushed windfalls on the ground, which seemed very far below me.'

'You didn't call for anyone?'

'I don't think it occurred to me. I think I made up my mind that the only way to do it was to jump.'

'Jump?'

'Yes. I saw all the branches criss-crossing, and the thick trunk below me, and the top of the ladder which I couldn't use because I couldn't get to it. So I closed my eyes and jumped.'

'Just threw yourself off?'

'A branch caught me under my chin, and I think it must have been that that snapped and cut my jaw.'

Valerian imagined her falling through the air. Again, he gently pressed the tip of his finger to the scar, near her jugular vein. She didn't flinch.

They were approaching the centre of the festival. People stared with greater concentration at Marion and drew aside to let her and Valerian pass. The crowd made a moving mass from which no one stood out, Valerian thought. He paused, Marion near him, and tried to look over the heads of the people for some point about which the festival revolved: a band, tables with food and drink, carnival booths for games, a decorated statue. There were none of these, however. The music came from loudspeakers attached to electricity poles. There was no way of knowing what the point of the festival was, really, except for the dense gathering.

Marion was jostled against him.

'Shall we leave?' he asked.

But she stood still. Coming straight towards her was an old man, his worn blue shirt open at the collar, his black suit baggy, his shoes falling apart; he was carrying a small branch. He stood before Marion, and with a smile that revealed gums and three yellow teeth, and that seemed to make all the wrinkles of his face radiate from about his eyes, he held out the branch to Marion. There was a moment when Valerian thought she was not going to take it, was going to turn away; he held his breath; she held out her hand for the branch, and the moment she grasped it the old man turned and left. A part of Valerian followed him, to hold him back and, with a gush of sentiment he knew was all out of proportion to the act, to embrace him. Immediately, though the people still ignored Valerian, they explained to Marion that behind the houses, near the school, was a demonstration of championship roller-skating.

They pressed their way to it. Next to the school was a basketball court, and around that was a low wall and a high chain-link fence. Valerian and Marion went up to the wall, along which people were standing : inside the court spectators were ranked on benches, and before them, in a spotlight, a girl on roller-skates was spinning.

At first she appeared as though multiplied, hundreds of static images of her following one after another in quick, then quicker and quicker sequence, until the images blurred together. The spectators clapped, and she spun even faster, the blurring, it seemed to Valerian, about to blur itself into nothing. Suddenly, with a clack, she was standing still, her arms raised. The crowd clapped again, and the girl, with a sidewards thrust of her body, curved off to the right on one skate.

Valerian looked from the girl to Marion, who was watching with great concentration, and a strange movement started up in him, or perhaps simply grew in impetus from feelings he had had all evening, all day, in one way or another, feelings that rose up in pity, and that were rising up now from deeper into a widening affection towards everything he saw around him – towards that girl, who was now skating backwards, her narrow pleated skirt flapping to reveal her white pants snug over her buttocks; towards the young man sitting on the wall, his shirt buttoned up to his neck, his black hair stiff and as if cut by blunt shears, dark rings around his eyes; towards a man standing beside Marion, a little girl riding on his hip, his eyes young, his cheeks furrowed with wrinkles; towards the shoes of the children standing on the wall; towards the stones of the wall – everyone, everything, so exposed, so open to some hideous silent violence over which no one, nothing, had any control.

He wanted to say, Oh, protect yourselves!

It seemed to him he must get away from the basketball court as quickly as possible. He stepped away and Marion stepped with him.

He asked, 'Would you prefer to stay?'

She shook her head.

He said, 'She's beautiful, the girl skating.'

'Yes,' Marion said.

They walked back to the village crossroads. People smiled as they passed through. Marion dangled her branch. All the eyes, the mouths, the hands Valerian saw drew from him more and more affection, and he thought: he must check it, he mustn't make a fool of himself – though he had no idea what form the affection might take that would make a fool of him. A woman touched Marion's arm and pointed to a pole on which some fireworks had been tied and a Catherine-wheel nailed. She raised four fingers of one hand and five of the other to indicate what time the fireworks would be lit. Three other people aided the woman in getting the point across.

'We'll have to stay,' Valerian said.

'Yes,' she answered.

'Do you mind?'

'No,' she said.

They wandered around. They were told often that there would be fireworks. In the shop in the village, tonic and wine was being sold. Valerian bought two paper cups of wine which they drank standing beneath a row of hanging sausages, among burlap bags of dried beans. They were told by the shopkeeper when the fireworks were about to be lit.

Over the heads, Valerian saw someone approach the pole with a burning candle. He touched the flame to a wick, waited, but nothing happened; he touched it again, waited, and a rocket shot up into the sky, fire streaming behind it, and exploded high above into a number of bright green lights which in turn exploded into showers of falling red sparks. A movement passed through Valerian that he found difficult to suppress; he wanted to exclaim, to release something of what he felt, with a round, open *Ah!*

A few other rockets were shot off. One didn't explode. The Catherine-wheel was ignited; it wobbled on its pivot, its streams of incandescent sparks undulating; it appeared about to fly off. Those spectators nearest it pulled back, laughing. The burning circle it created seemed to Valerian to be in him, where, too, it was about to fly out. Marion was standing just before him. He put a hand on her shoulder. She stepped backwards towards him and leaned against him, and he slid his arm over her shoulder across her chest; he pressed her closer to him, and she didn't resist. The wheel flared. He thought: protect yourselves! protect yourselves! His arm tightened around Marion. The humming wheel went out of focus through a film of tears. Its rockets flashed with a last thrust, the wheel spun uncertainly, then the rockets sputtered and died. Valerian released Marion, and they walked through the crowd that was already dispersing.

'Where is your branch?' Valerian asked.

She looked at her empty hands. 'I don't know.'

'Shall I look for it?'

'No,' she said.

'It'll only take me a second.'

'No. I don't want it. I want to leave it.'

As they passed the last house in the village, he noticed an old woman sitting on the door stoop. Her face was wrinkled as if a network of fine wires had been pressed into her flesh; her cheeks were hollow; she was toothless. She was sitting with her legs stretched out, and on her lap was a tin plate of cooked beans. She held the edge of the plate with one hand and with the other ate the beans with a big spoon in the way a child would eat by inserting the front of the spoon as deeply into her mouth as she could. She saw Valerian watching her, and she looked down, but nevertheless brought another spoonful of beans to her mouth. Her hand clutching the spoon was trembling. Tears streamed down his face at the sight of her.

He heard Marion ask, 'Is there anything wrong?'

He shook his head. He wanted to say, Oh, please, protect yourself.

She went to bed before he did. He sat outside. The night-time sky above him was immense. He easily identified constellations: the Great Bear, the Little Bear. The Milky Way was a swirling luminous vapour. Shooting stars streaked down.

She had not fallen asleep when he finally went to join her. The air in the room smelled of rosemary. He wondered if she had been lying awake thinking.

He said, after a moment, 'Perhaps you should leave me.'

'Why?'

'Because it's dangerous to stay.'

She said, 'No, I don't want to go.'

They fell asleep, or part of him fell asleep. Another part of him rose through the darkness and looked down at them both

147

in the bed. That part looked around the room, but couldn't see the walls, the floor, the ceiling, but stars in the night sky. He made out a mirror, then a comb on the bureau, then a slipper, but there appeared to be an infinite space around each object, and what the slipper had to do with the comb, or the comb with the mirror, was beyond him. He looked down at himself and Marion again, her mouth, his temple, his hand on her shoulder, their faces inclined towards one another.

Alone, she heard her voice ring sharply in her mind: 'What is it?' She almost hit the side of her head to knock the thought out of her mind.

She shook the colander. She removed a shrivelled black chick-pea that rose to the surface. She dropped it among other bad ones on a plate; it clicked.

She sensed Valerian standing at the kitchen door watching her. She didn't turn around. She hooked her heels over the chair rung, placed the colander in her lap, and leaned over it. She turned the peas over with her fingers. Under close examination, there appeared to be something wrong with every one of them: a dark spot, a dent. She heard Valerian approach. She felt like an exposed space trying to enclose itself, trying to encircle itself with boundaries across which he wouldn't step. But he stepped across. He put his hand on her shoulder.

'Wouldn't you like to go out?' he asked.

'No,' she said.

'We could go to the sea.'

'No.'

He sat on a chair before her. 'Let me help you with those.'

'You don't have to,' she answered, almost throwing the colander on the table, so a few peas jumped out; 'they've been picked over.'

He leaned towards her, one hand extended as if to take hold of her hands. He said, 'I wish you wouldn't close yourself off so –'

She didn't answer. She sat still.

His hand remained extended. 'Why don't you come with me?'

'Where?'

'Does it matter? We could go for a walk. We could go into town and have a coffee.'

'No,' she said. Her head lowered, she saw his hand approaching nearer hers, clenched in her lap.

He sat, 'You're more edgy than ever.'

'I am?'

'You think I'm going to do something to you, don't you?'

She stood, and Valerian did also.

'What could you do to me?' she asked.

Valerian said nothing.

Marion suddenly reached for the colander filled with chick-peas and threw it. It hit the bottle of olive oil which fell over; the oil made glug glug sounds as it poured out over the table. The peas showered everywhere.

Valerian left the kitchen. His shoes crunched peas.

Marion sat. The oil dripped from the table to the floor. She let it drip. She put her hands to her head. She thought: if she could only go all the way, further than she had ever been. What stopped her? What got in the way? Not Valerian – he wanted her to die. Why couldn't she break what stopped her? Why couldn't she say to Valerian, 'For God's sake, kill me.'?

She mopped up the oil. It took a long time. The rag she used spread the slippery puddle. She set a bowl of hot water and soap on the floor and rinsed the rag. She had to change the water often. Then she collected the chick-peas, one by one, from the floor, the table, the sink.

She hurried out to find Valerian. He was reading. He didn't put the book down, but she saw his eyes glance up quickly at her.

She said, 'Let's go out. Let's go for a walk.'

He didn't answer.

Her voice rose. 'Valerian!'

He looked up at her.

'Let's go out.'

'No,' he said.

A frightened aggressiveness came over her. She asked, 'Won't you come out?'

'No.'

'I'll go out myself,' she said.

'If you want.'

'You won't come with me?'

'No.'

She held back for a moment, then, with a kind of blind thrust, said, 'I'm going out. I'm going now.'

He laid the book face-down on his lap. He said firmly, 'Go. Go.'

She stood stark still. He had immobilized her; she didn't know how to move, and to be able to, he would have to tell her.

'Go,' he said again.

She had to think to make her body turn away from him, and when she got to the door she wondered how she could get through it. She knew he was watching her. She was like a patient unexpectedly dismissed from a hospital who stood at the entrance, unable to recall how to walk, and none of the nurses standing about, reflected in the highly polished floors, would help her. She stepped out.

The air was dead, the heat hard. The garden was as if embedded in the heat. Unseen, heat bugs trilled and rasped. She went to the gate and leaned over. The rutted dirt road, with its stone walls on either side, was like a dry river-bed; the heat lay heavily over it. Marion pushed open the gate and went out.

Her legs were stiff, her whole body rigid with the awareness that she had not wanted to come out, but having defied Valerian had forced herself out. She stood in the middle of the road. She wondered which way she should go.

She turned towards the village, though she didn't know what she would do there. She thought: her walk was pointless, and yet she was trying to make a point of it to show

Valerian – Dust rose in sluggish clouds around her espadrilles which made soft sounds as she walked.

The village appeared closed up and deserted. It was as if everyone in it had left because it was about to be attacked by men who were at this moment hiding behind rocks and walls in the wide, rocky landscape surrounding the village, and she was caught outside. They watched her, expecting her to make a gesture that would reveal that she knew they were there – suddenly running or crouching behind a wall. If she could simply stand, she thought; or, better, if she could go out to meet them. But she couldn't; she couldn't. They exposed her from all sides, knew her, had seen her do strange and uncontrollable things; they knew her intention to appear stark, untouched was half broken under their constant surveillance; they saw she wouldn't be able to hold out, and they were simply waiting for her to do something, because, caught among them, she would do something.

The door of the little grocery was open behind its chain fly-curtain, she noted. She went inside. The dim shop was empty. It smelled of cheese and pepper. She studied a cardboard box filled with meringues. The woman came in from the back and, completely without expression, looked at Marion. Marion stared at her for a moment. Marion asked for a meringue. Unsmiling, silent, the woman gave her one, took the money, then left. Alone, Marion ate the meringue. It was stale. Leaving the shop, she thought: she would go back to the house.

Just as she stepped into the road, she saw from the corner of her eye a figure dart behind the wall of a house diagonally across the road, and she knew, even before registering the fact visually, that it was Valerian. She felt the roots of her hair seem to move, and a prickling started there that swiftly spread into her neck, across her shoulders, down her back, throughout her body, to the tips of her breasts.

After a moment, she turned in the opposite direction from him and began walking through the village. All the shutters and doors were shut. There was no one else about. She walked slowly, the prickling sensation shooting through her each time it came to her that Valerian was behind her; she didn't turn round to look, but she could feel him, a presence pulling her back, and she walked ahead as though against the pull. She knew less than before what she should do.

At the edge of the village, she paused in the shade of a tree. The tree had large, pointed, yellowish leaves that were falling off. She jerked her head once towards the direction from which she had come, and saw, sticking from behind bales of hay piled up against a wall, his shoulder and arm. The prickling passed over her again. She continued out of the village.

She didn't want to go the way they usually went to the sea, imagining Valerian would assume that was where she would go. She turned off on to the unfamiliar path, the wheel ruts padded with straw-dry weeds. The path twisted and turned, sometimes passed houses behind high walls, as closed up as the houses in the village; it passed a wagon upside down and rotting; it passed a huge stone barn whose roof had fallen in; it passed a pile of broken roof tiles, then dwindled into an overgrown path through scrub. She thought: but even if she lost him, where would she go? Return to the house? She couldn't do that. She pushed aside some branches that grew across the path, and surrounded by the scrub she sat to get her breath back. The sunlight was shattered by the branches. It hurt her eyes to look up into it. She rested her forehead on her up-drawn knees. She could hear her pulse, and then, suddenly, she heard what sounded like one roof tile falling on another, and she was jolted up. She waited, facing the direction where he would come; when she heard, in the deep silence, dry weeds cracking, she turned, pushed her way out of the remaining scrub, and found herself at the edge of a large swelling field.

She had to climb a tumbled stone wall to get into it. It was used for grazing, but there were no animals in it, as there was nothing for the animals to feed on. It was larger than she had at first thought, for as she hurried over its swell, she could not see any other boundary walls. She didn't know which way to go. In the middle of the open field, she could go in any direction, she thought, and no matter what direction she took he would see her. She quickly turned back to look. The field was empty behind her. Heat waves rose in veils, distorting the yellow and ochre landscape. And then she saw him step from behind a tall wall and immediately step back.

She thought: he was pursuing her, and there was no place she could go to. If she ran, where would she run to? She started down the other side of the field's swell, which then slowly rose into a hill. She kept herself from looking behind. Climbing the hill was difficult. She felt she was pulling up all the field behind her. The hill, on the other side, fell away to a slope, and she gave into the declivity; it propelled her down to a stone house in ruins, three of its walls standing. She sat where the angle of two walls made a shadow. She could hear sea waves.

She got up after a brief pause and jumped over a low broken wall of the house, hurried across what had been the house's garden, down some stone steps, and was faced by a thick, wide wall of rushes and reeds. The ground was soft and wet.

She looked behind. The hill rose up; it appeared to her very high. Valerian came over the top and stood. He must have seen her, she thought, but he was no longer hiding from her. They had come too far, and he of course knew that she was aware he was following her; he had no reason to hide. She saw him start down the hill.

She thrust herself into the rushes and reeds. She found herself up to her ankles in water, and her espadrilles were sucked into soft black sand. She was standing in a stream. She followed it deeper into the reeds and rushes, where, in the hot, misty stillness, she heard only trickling water. She had to crouch down to follow the stream. The sand sucked at her espadrilles, which she had to pull off. She carried them.

She came out of the reeds on to a little cove and beach covered thick in banks of seaweed. The stream spread out into puddles or cut through the seaweed in deep, branching rivulets that flowed down to the sea. The sea was low, blanketed in a sheen of light, its waves in the cove thin and slurring, as though it had silenced itself because of her intruding presence. She did feel that she was intruding, that a second before she had come something had quickly disappeared into the sea, and was floating just beneath the surface, waiting for her to go away. The isolation, the silence of the place pressed the feeling more deeply on her.

She moved quickly to the side of the beach where she saw a zigzagging path leading up the side of a steep, rocky incline. She put on her wet espadrilles to climb. Half way up, she looked back to catch Valerian breaking his way through the reeds. His hair was dishevelled. He didn't look around for her, but went to the sea, took off his sandals, and plunged in.

She paused to stare down at him, and the sight of him swimming in the sea, distant from her, suddenly broke her urge to continue climbing; she wondered why she was running away from him. It came to her for a moment that they could both detach themselves from what they were, from what they were doing, from everything that had happened, and, as matter-of-factly as Valerian now swam in the sea, they could quite simply meet, they could – She felt a kind of shift in her heart as she watched Valerian emerge from the sea, his shorts and shirt dark and sagging with water; she wanted to run down to him, to say, 'Oh yes, oh yes!'

He put on his sandals and slowly came across the beach towards her, as if he knew everything they had gone through was over now, that she was simply waiting for him.

But, staring at him, a moment later she continued up the path to the top of the headland.

It was covered with close-growing wild rosemary. The branches scraped across her legs and arms. She was arrested by a huge spider-web; she backed away and took another route among the short, gnarled, tough bushes, odorous in the enveloping heat.

In the distance was a small building, grey-white. She went to it. Its door and one small window were broken in. Inside, amidst torn nets and smashed lobster traps, she leaned against a wall. Across from her, the window framed Valerian advancing. The sight of him made her quickly leave the building; she didn't want him to find her inside. Outside, she could at least run from him.

There was not much further to go, however. The headland ended in a point, a promontory whose jagged edge fell away to the sea. She looked over the edge; waves, far below, broke against the rocks. She turned. Valerian was close enough for her to see his expression. He didn't look straight at her; he peered up at her from his lowered head. Ten feet away from her, he stopped.

It was only when she saw he was panting that she realized she, too, was panting. His wild hair made her put her hands to her head to find that hers was wild. She wanted to sit, to lie down, but she remained fixed, staring at him. Her mind went in and out, the landscape went in and out, in and out, heaving with her breathing. Valerian took a step nearer, and she felt everything about her spin into fragments and a confusion of thoughts and feelings in the midst of which she could not know what was happening or what he wanted. The confusion made her eyes go out of focus as he came closer to her, passed her, and went to the edge; he now appeared to be at a great distance. He looked over, down to the rocks and the sea.

He turned back and came up to her. She suddenly saw his face very close up. Sweat was streaking down his temples and cheeks. His voice made a dry, low sound. 'Why don't you do something?' he asked.

She remained still.

'Why don't you help me in what I can't bear any longer?'

She tried to look at him.

'That I love you, that I love you, that I love you.'

Her voice was very small. 'You want not to?'

'Yes, yes. It's death.'

'For you?'

'For us both.'

She said nothing.

Sweat dripped over his brows; his face shone. 'You won't love me?'

She took a tiny step backward. 'You couldn't make me.'

'In no way.'

Her heart, she felt, was about to burst. 'No, in no way.'

He looked at her. He said, 'Of course you're right. I should have seen from the first. I shouldn't have done anything but leave you alone, as you were, as you are now.' He paused. Drops ran down his face. 'Perhaps it isn't too late.'

Too late? she thought. Her eyes followed the movements of his lips. She understood his words, but she wasn't sure she understood what they were saying all together; she had a sense she wouldn't like what they were saying all together, a sense that brought with it a panic which, in its first stirring, seemed to her would go deeper, would erupt more violently than the panic she had felt when she believed he was going to pick her up and fling her over the edge; she felt it move beneath his words.

She heard her voice say, 'You can't leave.'

His brows knitted together. 'I can't?'

'No,' she said.

His eyes were steady on her. 'I can,' he said quietly.

'No. You know you can't. You were never able to. But now, more than ever, you can't.'

His voice remained quiet. 'Why?'

Her voice shot off. 'Because of what you promised me!'

He said nothing.

'You can't leave without showing me what you promised me! You can't do that! No, no!' She went closer to him. Her voice came from her in a low, hoarse whisper; it was the voice of someone else. 'Show me!'

He closed his eyes for a second. She thought he would fall over. He opened his eyes and looked past her, and she saw in them that he knew whatever little personal gesture he made would not change anything. She saw him look over the sky, wincing as his eyes passed the sun. He moved away from her and went to the edge of the promontory.

She was going to go up to him, but she saw him step closer to the edge. As though she could draw him away by pulling against him with the weak gravity of her body, she stepped back from him.

'Come away,' she said.

He turned to her slowly so as not to lose his balance. He smiled.

'Come away,' she repeated.

He didn't move.

She continued to pull against him, feeling the tension. She said, 'You wouldn't do it.'

'That's because you don't believe me,' he said. 'If you told me to, I would.'

'No, you wouldn't.'

'Tell me.'

She felt her body sway with the pull and sudden little releases of tension, that, caught up, jerked her forward.

'Tell me.'

She heard the waves breaking far below.

'Tell me,' he said.

She held herself steady.

He rocked slightly. 'Tell me.'

As if, all at once, he gave a yank to a tense wire that held them together, so it went slack, and she lost the pull, lost it so that she imagined it had snapped, she felt a gap, and in the gap she knew that if she told him, yes, do it, he would throw himself over, knew that he was more than taking a risk, he was insisting she tell him. And then, it was as if, for a second, she said, yes, do it, do it, and he fell, fell soundlessly, and she saw break open before her the terror of everything in her that was beyond her.

Her panic seized her. She lunged towards him, pushing him and at the same time grabbing his legs and pulling. They lost balance and landed backwards on the ground where, her body trembling from the impact, she began to beat him, to beat him wildly, and to scream.

He lay still.

Marion got up and walked away from him, though she could hardly stand or lift her feet over the rocks sticking up from the ground. She felt that a long, heavy tense cord in her, running from the vast inner sounding space of her skull to the top of her spine, had been drawn out like the string of an immense bow, drawn out as far as it could go, then suddenly released, and the vibrations in the cord were knocking her from side to side, were making her shake to her fingertips and toes. She sat on the ground. She drew up her knees and tightened her arms around them. There was nothing she could do but sit and wait for the vibrations to diminish. But they went on; the more she tightened her arms about her knees the more she trembled, until she had to remove her arms from her knees and let the trembling take over.

She saw an insect crawling over the parched ground, she saw a rusty bent nail, she saw a broken shell.

Still trembling, she got up. She looked around to where she had left Valerian. He was, as before, lying on the ground, face up. His eyes were closed. She went to him and crouched beside him. She could see the pulse pumping in his neck. She said:

'We must go back.'

He didn't move.

'You can't lie like this in the sunlight,' she said. 'We must go.'

He said nothing, but got up. He didn't look at her.

She led the way across the headland and down the zigzagging path to the beach. Instead of following her across the beach, however, Valerian went to the edge of the water. Marion stopped and watched him. He walked back and forth at the edge, where the flat, spreading waves covered his feet and sandals. He walked back and forth quickly. Marion took a few steps towards him, but stopped.

She waited. As sharply as he had gone to the edge of the water, he came back to her. She followed him over the banks of seaweed to the opening in the patch of reeds and rushes through which the stream ran. She took off her espadrilles before going in.

She said, 'You'd better take off your sandals.'

'It doesn't matter,' he answered.

'They'll be ruined, and you've just had them repaired.'

He took them off.

They bent down to walk in the bed of the stream through the massed reeds.

On the other side, Valerian only paused to put on his sandals. He walked on as if he had no intention of stopping until he reached their house. Marion didn't think she would be able to walk all the way back across the fields, along the dirt roads, to the house. The hill before her appeared enormous.

'I must rest,' she said.

There was nothing in Valerian's voice to indicate that he was tired, or that he couldn't, by sheer insistence, walk past their house, to the port, and on to the next boat going out.

'You can rest in those ruins,' he said.

Marion sat in the corner of two remaining walls of the house where she had sat before. While she sat, Valerian wandered about the stones. He descended a flight of steps to a lower level, which might have been a granary or mill, for she could see in the midst of the rubble of broken stones and timbers and plaster a worn millstone. Valerian was poking around the rubble with a stick. Perhaps, she thought, he was trying to kill lizards. She watched him.

Marion closed her eyes, but listening to the scraping heat bugs, a gurgle of distant water, a gull, she imagined that when she opened her eyes she would see that Valerian had disappeared or had become a little baby or even a fish flopping madly, beating itself on the hot stones. She heard a soft thud, like a fish thrashing; it must have been Valerian striking a lizard. She kept her eyes closed.

She pressed her back against the stone wall, against its hardness and thickness. She felt herself caught up and swiftly brought back to the promontory, felt the black sunlight, and Valerian balanced on the edge, and her voice breaking out of her lungs: Oh yes! Again, a violent tremor passed through her. She opened her eyes. She saw at her feet a chunk of plaster; she was amazed that it should lie so very still.

She looked up after a while to see Valerian peeing over a broken wall. His pee, flashing in the sunlight, arched the wall.

They walked side by side, not talking. Why, she wondered, did she find it impossible to say, 'There is a sheep, there is a horse,' ignoring all the vagueness, the inarticulateness of what had happened for two or three facts? Why couldn't she turn to Valerian and, as if seeing him for the first time, say, 'It's hot,' and that would be all, that would be all there was to consider? No. In her and around her, in the air, on the ground, lay an infinite anonymous chaos of objects that she had never thought of together, of relations that had never attracted her attention, and she knew the most startling conjunction of those objects was herself and Valerian now walking silently side by side. All her smallest motions were in harmony with his, her right arm swinging past his left arm swinging in the opposite direction, their left feet, then right, touching the ground at the same moment, the slight swaying movements of their shoulders and hips, and her concentration on their motions kept making more and more connections between their fingers, necks, eyes, until all the connections, she thought, built up an incalculable complexity of patterns which she realized she was just beginning to be aware of, patterns which she saw extend from her eye to a snail shell, from the snail shell to a bit of rope it adhered to, from the bit of rope to Valerian's eye which she saw glance from it to a distant large boulder, from a bird alighting on the boulder back to her eye, and nothing, nothing, could be isolated from the midst, as she and Valerian now could not be isolated from the massively complex act of walking together, from the air and the landscape around them, as if, in a flash, a world, had confused itself together about them, and they couldn't escape it. She didn't want to escape it, and, with a sudden recognition that made her want to tell Valerian, though she knew she could not, she knew she had never wanted to escape it.

Once inside the house, he stayed away from her. Marion showered, spread cream over the scratches and bruises on her arms and legs, combed out her wet hair and pulled it back tightly. She dressed. She lay on the divan in the sitting-room while Valerian used the bathroom. He was there a long time. The evening dusk deepened. She rose when he came out, drying himself; without looking at her, he crossed into the bedroom and shut the door.

She remained on the couch. She heard him go into the kitchen, perhaps to eat. Then she heard him go upstairs into the room Ronald had used. After a while, she got up and went into the bedroom.

She lay across the bed dressed as she was. She knew he would spend the night up there, and all the following nights. She saw them, one after another, like black veils, and as many as she pulled back she was not able to get to the end of them. She fell asleep pulling them aside.

Her body ached in the morning. Moving stiffly, she levered herself up from the bed. When she opened the door to the sitting-room, she saw Valerian on the divan. He was asleep. She walked gently and sat across from him. His eyes were open in slits, and his lids were quivering. His mouth was open. His arms were clutched about him as if he might be chilly. From the bedroom, she pulled a thin blanket off the bed and brought it into the sitting-room to cover him. He stirred a little, his lips opened more and closed, then he lay motionless.

She went to the toilet, then came back to sit and watch him. She didn't want him to wake. When he did, she jumped up and pretended to be crossing the room. At the door, however, she looked back. He was looking at her. She said:

'I was about to go for the milk.'

He simply nodded.

The old hunchbacked woman filled the milk pail from a bucket with a ladle. The milk frothed.

When she got back to the house, she found the divan empty, and the blanket lay rumpled on the floor.

He kept away from her for the rest of the day. He didn't leave the house, but moved to another room if she came into the one he was in, as though she could do something to him if he stayed, and it occurred to her, with a great internal swelling of all her massed feelings, what she had done: she had told him to jump, and he had.

Marion woke to a morning grey with low-lying clouds. The air was very still and saturated as with steaming hot water.

When she saw Valerian, she suggested they should hire a car and drive to the other side of the island. Valerian neither agreed nor disagreed.

The car was covered with a fine layer of wet dust. Marion drew circles in it, waiting for Valerian to join her.

She drove. The landscape unfolded past Valerian, her, the car: long flat planes, grey-white and black.

He was, she thought, as if submerged in water, and at no point – tips of fingers, toes, back, buttocks – was he in touch with objects. They floated just beyond his reach. He showed no interest in reaching them or touching them in any case.

Marion pointed out things: a white village on a hill that rose from a wide plain, an old tree, a cow.

He saw them, but they floated away from his vision as if on running water.

Marion had difficulty driving the car. The gears ground; every time she changed them, the car shuddered. She drove slowly, trying to point out whatever she could see in the dry landscape to interest him. She wasn't sure he took in anything she did point out. He remained silent.

Now and then she had to stop the car by the side of the road to check the map. Twice she'd taken the wrong road, and had to turn round. She asked Valerian to guide her, but he held the map open on his knees and didn't look at it. When she asked him if they were headed in the right direction, he said he was not sure. She stopped the car again. It took her a long time to figure out where they were. Her only indication was a red spot on the map that marked a prehistoric site; to the left, in a field, was a high mound at the base of which stood a large stone hut or tomb; she imagined that must have been the site. She orientated herself, and drove off.

The town she chose to go to had, like the town nearest where they lived, a port, but it was small and unused. This town was older, too; it looked as though it had been flooded for years and years, and after the water receded nothing was done to repair the walls, the roofs. The narrow streets smelled of fish.

Marion led Valerian from where she had parked the car – which had given a last great shudder when she shut off the ignition – down through the streets to the port. She kept turning to look at his eyes, hoping they were taking in everything they passed, but his eyes appeared glazed. He saw nothing.

The restaurant she chose for lunch was on the quai. A cat sat under their table. Marion ordered. The waiter, an old man who appeared to have just got up from a long sleep with his clothes on, turned to Valerian. Valerian held the menu up before him, but he was not reading, Marion saw.

'Why don't you order the same as I?' she asked.

'Yes,' Valerian said.

She told the waiter. The food was a long time coming. The waiter served it as though he were still half asleep.

She saw, watching him eat, that he didn't know the forkful of food he was lifting to his mouth had anything to do with him, as if there were even a distance between himself and those functions that kept him alive, a great circular distance which nothing could penetrate. When he drank wine, some spilled over the rim and ran down from the side of his mouth.

She dreaded the end of the meal, and tried to think ahead what they might do after, though Valerian didn't show that he wanted to leave; in fact, he drank his coffee slowly.

They walked about the town after.

Some streets were too narrow for cars, and they narrowed even more as they entered a quarter where the houses appeared older and more sea-eroded than the rest of the town. The air, too, seemed heavier, and the smells of fish and seaweed made her think that the sea was still flooding the cellars and tunnels and foundations of these buildings. The people looked away as Marion and Valerian passed.

They climbed a steep street. At the top was what appeared to be a courtyard, with the backs of high buildings crowded around it, and between the buildings were flights of steps. Water ran down the closest flight. Marion went to the next, Valerian behind her. They went by open doors, and through them she saw into rooms, and rooms behind rooms, and all the rooms were empty.

Through an open doorway she saw a young man and woman standing together in a bare room. The young man and woman had evidently stopped what they were doing to stare at Marion and Valerian as they passed. Marion exchanged brief looks with them; their eyes were large, dark, filled with some deep soft inner preoccupation that left Marion out entirely.

The image of the couple stayed with her, their clothes old and loose, standing in the deeply shadowed room with a stone floor, looking at one another, then, for a moment, staring out of the doorway at Marion and Valerian passing, two strangers, whose relationship was to the couple's eyes so far outside what they knew as to be unimaginable.

At the top of the flight of stairs was a slit-like passage. Marion went ahead. She came out into a small square. One side of the square was taken up by a building with a portico. The door under the portico was open. It was a museum.

The small rooms were cluttered with fragments of carvings, with shattered pots badly pieced together, with corroded knife blades and axe-heads. Marion drew Valerian from glass case to

164

glass case, but he simply stood behind her, looking nowhere in particular. She kept trying to find one object that would take his interest. Her fingernail tapped on the glass when she pointed out a little round bowl, but he was turned the other way.

She suddenly couldn't bear to be with him. She went into another room. His heavy presence, disassociated from the bone tools, shaped flints, arrow heads, had a margin about it which made it impossible for anything to touch him. She wouldn't be able to touch him. He followed her into the room, but stood in the middle. She didn't know what to do. She again left him.

She went into a little cloister. She was sure he would follow her out in a moment. Around the inner walls of the cloister were dirty broken stone memorial plaques. The paving was dirty also, she had to avoid heaps of dust. She saw, sticking from a heap of dust, a pottery fragment, and reached down to pick it up. Blowing the dust from it revealed part of a meander. She turned the shard over and over in her fingers, wondering what shape the pot had had. She tried to reconstruct a shape, and as she did she suddenly, abruptly sobbed. She threw the shard down.

Valerian was in the doorway to the cloister waiting for her. She could hardly keep herself from sobbing against him.

The hot inside air of the car smelled of gasoline. She thought it was perhaps because the car had been closed, but when she tried to start it there was only a clacking sound and the smell of gasoline increased.

She waited, tried again, and nothing happened. She and Valerian sat in silence, then she tried again, and still nothing happened. She opened the door for air. 'We'll have to get help,' she said. A group of children had surrounded the car.

They led her and Valerian to the one garage in the town. A man came to look. Nothing could be done before the next day.

With relief, Marion said, 'We'll have to spend the night.'

There were two beds in the hotel room. She kicked off her sandals and lay on one. In the middle of the ceiling was a dim light-bulb that projected needles of light; the rest of the room was almost in darkness. Valerian, by his bed, was undressing. She could not see him clearly, but his torso emerged, pale in the dimness, and she imagined she could smell an odour from it that had become familiar to her : a muskiness, a smell as of some pungent crushed plant. She tried to breathe it in. He stepped around his bed, passed her, and went to the window to open the shutters.

She became aware of her clothes tightening against her. Her breasts, her thighs, seemed to swell. When he turned around from the window and faced her, making her think for a moment he was going to come to her, a twinge passed through her; she sensed constraints all about her, and had to change her position. She could see his shoulders, his arms. He raised an arm to brush his hair back from his forehead. She saw – or imagined she saw – the muscles move.

He stood immobile. She wondered if he were waiting for her to do something. She slowly swung her legs over the side of the bed and sat on the edge. She heard her own breathing. He remained where he was. She stood and quickly threw off her clothes, but when she was naked she felt as exposed as if she were standing on the street; she sat and drew her legs together. He took a step, and her toes, heels, calves of her legs, knees, fingertips, palms, elbows, chin, nipples, navel suddenly became points in an outward attention to him. Every part of her was aware of him, and when he took another step she had to restrain herself from jumping up to meet him.

She sat still, and he crossed the room to his bed. He pulled back the blankets and lay on his back. He flicked a switch on a cord above his headboard and shut off the light.

Marion watched him across the space between the two beds.

All at once, she swiftly rose, her feet hardly touching the floor, and lay beside him. The weight of his body made the mattress sink in. She was rolled against his long naked side.

She wished she could slide under him, under his weight, so she'd be pressed hard into the mattress. She put her hand on the middle of his chest, and he turned away.

After a while, she got up and went to her own bed.

In the darkness, she heard all around her sounds which she could not identify, for even if she thought, that was water rushing over rocks, she knew there was no stream within miles of her. She could, at times, make out voices, but she had no idea who might be speaking, or what they were saying, or in what language. The voices might have come from auditory recollections of the people she had heard during the day speaking in restaurants, cafés, on the street, as there was no one near enough to her now to be heard. Then she thought: perhaps the voices were not voices, but other sounds that had the tones of voices, short variously pitched beeps that were like words. She listened.

The sounds filled the darkness, and she lay deep within them as in the midst of a rich sonic confusion. All the while she listened, she thought:

Valerian, Valerian.

She saw herself standing above him, above his dead body. She saw herself trying to make love to him, as he lay, dead, on her, so weighty it was difficult for her to move, and though she embraced him as tightly as she could, kissed him, biting and sucking his lips, kissed his face with a vehemence that would have her kissing through flesh to his skull, everything straining in her to bring him back, she knew that she would not.

She heard, suddenly, a muffled sound from Valerian. She rose up on her elbows. She couldn't see him. Her ears became enormous in her attempt to hear him, but she couldn't even make out his breathing. She lay back.

She thought: no, she didn't want to die.

Her body urged her to get up, to light the light, to wake him, but what kept her flat and motionless was the fear that they were no longer in the hotel room.

She lay rigid, sensing the space around them grow and

deepen, and there was nothing in it that was familiar, nothing in it that had anything to do with her thinking and feeling, for they had both passed through an unnoticed, open moment, as empty as zero, and nothing of what they knew on the side of the room with its beds and tables and chairs remained.

She was not sure she woke or became suddenly aware of the dawn rising dimly. She realized there was complete silence.

She turned her head. As if she had forgotten him, Valerian appeared to her, stretched out face up on his bed, his eyes closed, his mouth slightly agape. She noted his arms, his feet sticking out from the sheet, his hair, the darkness of beard.

When, as though he were aware she was looking at him, he turned on his side towards her and for a brief second opened his eyes and looked at her, everything in Marion, everything that kept her still rigid, broke, and through her and around her poured a sense that rose and rose, which she tried to keep up to as it rushed on and on, but there was nothing she could grasp of it.

She got up and went into the bathroom. She stood before the basin and splashed water over her face. Glancing in the mirror, the image held her. She looked at the cheeks, the hair, the eyes. They were not her cheeks, her hair, her eyes, The eyes that looked back at her were the eyes of someone she didn't know. She continued to stare, to examine those eyes examining her. The large black pupils were deep holes.

An image occurred to her suddenly, spontaneously, of herself and Valerian, tangled in one another's arms, falling, falling down a black hole, falling deeper and deeper, falling beyond hot and cold, beyond light and darkness, falling and falling until, without knowing when it happened, they found they were slowly rising.

Valerian's white body rose in the darkness.

Marion walked back and forth, back and forth, in the red light, while he remained still, staring at her. She stared at him also, didn't take her eyes from him while pacing from end to end of the long patch of light.

When he looked down, he saw the curved planes of his chest, of stomach and thighs, saw nipples, navel, his cock; far below, he saw feet. The body appeared very white. He saw a hand rise and touch the middle of the chest, then, with just the tips of his fingers, slide down to the stomach.

He was dimly aware of a long column in him – perhaps his spinal column – that drew in the sliding sensation of the fingers against the skin from the surface of his body to itself where, as about a pole, the sensations revolved. He scratched a knee, and that sensation, too – the sensation of both the itch and his scraping his fingernails – was drawn inside to revolve about his spine. He scratched a buttock, he ran a hand the length of the opposite arm, sweat trickled under an armpit.

Slight draughts seemed to circulate about him and play on the area beneath a collarbone, on the left side of his waist, about the calf of his right leg, on his nape, along his left fore-arm, as if thin layers of skin were pulled off here and there, exposing him to the air. He couldn't stand much longer here, he thought, and yet he didn't move.

He watched Marion walk back and forth, back and forth. She wouldn't come nearer. When she raised her hands, touched her hair, moved her fingers, he wondered if she were gesturing to him.

She saw him through the diffused light. He stood leaning at a slight angle towards her, as though poised. His arms hung to his sides; they swung a little. She had no idea what she must do to get him over, but she would do it, would pull him if she must by nothing but her desire to pull him.

He stood back, but he was aware that he was watching her with a kind of awe as her breasts swayed slightly, her thighs pivoted. The light, he thought, was a red skin around her, and it made her nudity appear a thin cover to a deeper nudity, a nakedness beneath the light which, when revealed, would ex-pose her to a rawness of blood and heat. He imagined himself touching the skin of light, and it would, like tissue, adhere to his fingertips and tear away.

A slight jerk of his muscles impelled his hands to tear it away, tear it off.

He rubbed his palms against his chest, as if wiping them against his skin.

The light, as she moved, moved over her, so the luminous skin appeared loose, and again he felt his fingers reaching out to pull it off. She turned completely about, her back towards him, and it came to him, for a second, that he might quickly approach her without her knowing it, and, swiftly reaching for her shoulders, strip her.

When she turned to him, that long column in him shook with his suddenly confronted longing to expose her possession like a fresh wound.

Oh no, he thought –

But the sensations he felt emanating from her – from her forehead, her nose, her nipples, her navel – shot out and penetrated through him, billowing in wide circles and winding around his spine, drawing him so close he would wound her with the angles of his body. Her kneecaps moved, her fingers curled and uncurled, she blinked rapidly.

She smiled. She raised a hand, and with a slight twist of her body appeared to take a dance step. He took a step backward, stopped.

He had no idea how he got to her. All he knew was the pressure of her breasts, stomach, thighs expanding against him; his glans pressed into her tickling pubic hair. She held him and, her mouth open as if to speak, kissed him. The inside wetness of her lips circled his mouth; her breath was warm. He hardly moved. She kissed him on the neck, on his shoulders; she drew back to kiss his chest, and lowered her head to suck, with soft warm contractions of her lips, at one of his nipples. She touched the nipple with her tongue, and his body buckled with the contact. He straightened up, and suddenly drew her closer to him to kiss her, kiss her forehead, eyes, to lick the lobes of her ears, the base of her throat. He felt her body contract with each kiss, as if they were painful to her.

She clasped her hands around his neck, and pressed closer to him. She swung her legs up around his waist and, with a passion to outdo the pain of his kisses, kissed him in return. He staggered.

He sank to his knees, then they rolled over, her legs still around him, their arms around each other; they rolled over and over, rolled from side to side, kissing wherever they could reach, as if they were trying to encircle each other with kisses.

When they stopped, they fell apart. He could feel her arm across his chest, heavy immobile. He found her lying, face down, her hair hiding her face. He drew her hair away. Her face was smooth, clear, as if washed in water; drops rolled from her temple. Her throat, he noted, was round and full, like the throat of a child. She looked at him without moving.

He picked up the hand on his chest and kissed it, then laid it against his throat. He lifted himself on to his side. He pulled her slack body to him, and kissed her across her forehead.

Her forehead, he thought, was a clear rectangle, and as he studied her face all the planes of it simplified into geometric figures, as clear as glass.

She sat up. She brushed her hair away. She looked down at his body, at the square of his abdomen, the triangles of his chest, the interlocking circles of his thighs. She traced the lines with a finger.

They were quiet. The patch of red light had become a long low horizontal bar, and while they sat the bar blurred into a flesh pink.

She was outlining his body, he thought, as though it were hers, and she were determining the areas of it; in fact, it was hers, all the warm flesh and bone. She could do what she wanted to do. He grabbed the finger with which she was tracing patterns over him and, kissing it, put it in his mouth.

His tongue was wet and warm to her touch. She ran her fingers over it. She took the finger out, took hold of one of his hands, and, pressing the fingers into a fist, knocked her forehead with it.

171

He spread his fingers out and slid his hand to the back of her head, and pulled her down to kiss her softly.

She felt that she would pour out of her mouth, pour down into him and with another kiss it seemed to her a current was started in her, as though all her thoughts and feelings were rising in waves, and she must empty them all into him, into his mouth. A suffusion of warmth rose in her.

His chest suddenly seemed to be lifting itself up towards her. He pressed her back and lay on her. He kissed her along the jaw, on her temples, her cheeks, along the shoulders, between her breasts, across her waist, as if to press on her small delicate points that would, when connected, make up the imprint of his body.

The light paled, and they lay, still, in the darkness. He felt himself sink, then, with small jolts, suddenly rise.

She moved, her fingers touched his shoulder, then she was still once more. He knew she wasn't sleeping, though he wondered how he knew; he could only sense her staring awareness – perhaps she even had her eyes open, was staring out into the darkness.

His own awareness, running the sensitive length of his spine, registered what he realized was a sound when it finally became audible, a wind-like hum as of a slow, continuous movement in the dark.

Her fingertips moved against his shoulder.

Cadences detached themselves from the deepening sound, and he wasn't able to tell where they rose from. He listened, and, abruptly, calls came from somewhere, or perhaps they were little sonic bursts; they made her finger, touching him still, jump slightly with a start. He turned to her. He could barely make out her eyes.

Dark voices, he thought, would, like phrases repeated over and over again, work themselves into them as they lay. Even when he inserted a finger in his ears, as to unblock them from a change in pressure, the voices continued; and then, slowly,

172

they started to intone. He reached out and put a hand between her breasts.

Glowing shapes appeared before his eyes: the shape of her eyes, her nose, her chin.

He reached out with his other hand and drew her to him.

In his arms, she circled him with hers. As she couldn't see him, she wondered if it was in fact he, because each time she touched him there passed through her fingers the shock of touching someone for the first time. She touched his shoulders, his back, his thighs. He moved when she touched him, pressing her.

Her arms around him, she rolled over on to him. She kissed him. His body, stretched out beneath her, was heaving, and she thought: there was nothing else but his body, and maybe there wasn't even his body.

Music: oh yes, they were caught up by it, she thought, caught up and surrounded by it as by a landscape. They inhabited, both of them, a country of sound.

She kissed his ears. She kissed his temples. Her lips encountered wetness when she kissed the hollows around his eyes. Pulling her closer, he returned her kisses. Quickly, he shifted his position and wound his legs around hers. She tightened herself against him.

Through the darkness, the music kept rising. They were sure of nothing, not, finally, if she were lying on him or under him, or he on her or under her. Voices, now near, now far, seemed to them to echo, but they didn't know what they could echo against. When it came to them that they no longer knew if they were lying or upright, they clung more tightly to one another. They didn't understand their love-making as they didn't understand the music, the voices, as they didn't know if they were horizontal or upright, but if they were upright, they were dancing.